All I Want For Christmas

by Clare Lydon

custard books

First Edition October 2015
Published by Custard Books
Copyright © 2015 Clare Lydon
ISBN: 978-0-9933212-8-3

Cover Design: Kevin Pruitt
Editor: Laura Kingsley
Typesetting: Adrian McLaughlin

Find out more and sign up for my mailing list at:
www.clarelydon.co.uk
Follow me on Twitter: @clarelydon
Follow me on Instagram: @clarefic

All rights reserved. This book or any portion thereof may not be reproduced or used in any manner whatsoever without the express written permission of the author.

This is a work of fiction. All characters and happenings in this publication are fictitious and any resemblance to real persons (living or dead), locales or events is purely coincidental.

Also by Clare Lydon

The All I Want Series
All I Want For Valentine's (Book 2)
All I Want For Spring (Book 3)
All I Want For Summer (Book 4)
All I Want For Autumn (Book 5)
All I Want Forever (Book 6)

Other Novels
A Taste Of Love
Before You Say I Do
Nothing To Lose: A Lesbian Romance
Once Upon A Princess
The Long Weekend
Twice In A Lifetime
You're My Kind

The London Romance Series
London Calling (Book 1)
This London Love (Book 2)
A Girl Called London (Book 3)
The London Of Us (Book 4)
London, Actually (Book 5)
Made In London (Book 6)

ACKNOWLEDGEMENTS

I love Christmas, so this book was an absolute joy to write. But as with all books, I couldn't do it alone. I've got some brilliant friends and colleagues who helped me along the way, and an army of fabulous readers who encourage me to keep on writing. If you're one of those people, thank you so much — your support means the world to me.

Particularly, thanks to my beta readers Angela Peach, Tammara Adams & Rachel Batchelor. Your feedback made this a better book, as well as telling me when I was making up words or just plain using the wrong ones. You can't mow an ice rink? No, I suppose you're right. Thanks also to Hilary Sangster for her eagle eye, and to all my early readers for crucial feedback and corrections.

Huge plaudits to my amazingly talented cover designer Kevin Pruitt for what he rightly tells me is our cutest cover yet. I was panicking about this one, but you put an arm around me and delivered the goods. I owe you many beers. Oodles of thanks also to my typesetter and networking husband, Adrian McLaughlin, who works tirelessly for the payment of white wine. And a tip of the hat to my developmental editor Laura Kingsley for kicking my butt on this one and making it a way better book.

My wife Yvonne also puts up with me on every book journey, cajoling, patting my head and serving up fantastic dinners when I'm glued to the computer. Her steaks are still the best in town, best served with an Aussie red.

But mostly, thanks to you for reading this book and supporting my work. Writers can't be writers without readers, so thank you, thank you, thank you! Whisper it, but you're pretty damn awesome.

Connect with me:
Tweet: @clarelydon
Instagram: @clarefic
Email: mail@clarelydon.co.uk
Sign up for my mailing list at: www.clarelydon.co.uk

This novel is dedicated to you.
Thanks for buying the book & Happy Christmas!

1

Friday November 25th

"You know, I don't want a lot for Christmas." That was me, Tori Hammond saying that. Lover of all things Christmas and festive. Even I couldn't believe the words were coming from my mouth, but they were definitely mine.

"Thank you, Mariah." That was my best friend Holly replying.

I pulled my thick grey scarf around me and shivered in the early evening air. We were sat on our bench at the top of our hill, looking up at the charcoal sky. It had been our hill since school, where we'd met 16 years ago. As teenagers, Holly and I had sat and discussed boys here because we thought that's what we were meant to do. Now aged 27, we sat and bemoaned women and pretended our world had evolved.

Behind us was a path lined with bare chestnut trees, their leaves long since dropped. Ahead of us was the smudged outline of the city, fogging up with every breath we took.

"No, I mean it," I said, my breath a ghostly circle swirling in front of me. "I don't need any new clothes or shoes, jewellery or perfume. My mum keeps asking me what I want, and I don't know what to tell her."

Holly rapped her knuckles lightly on my skull. Her long legs were crossed, her green duffel coat done right up, her short dark hair peeking out of her hat on one side, part-shaved on the other. In the darkening light, her pointed features appeared almost sinister, but Holly was one of the kindest people I knew — she was anything but sinister.

"Hello, Earth to Tori — is that you or have you been taken over by some alien invaders? You love Christmas! You're the biggest Christmas lover I know."

I shrugged. "And that hasn't changed — Christmas is still my most favourite time of the year. I just don't want any big presents this time."

"I'll remind you of that when I give you nothing," Holly said. "You could tell your mum to give you a Good Gift — a goat for a family in Africa or something. My gran bought my mum the gift of sight for five children last year."

I turned my head. "How did she react?"

Holly smiled her lopsided smile. "Mum said it was a nice gesture, but a bottle of gin to go with it wouldn't have gone amiss."

I smiled as I turned to face front again, looking out over the city skyline that was twinkling in the inky gloom before me. "Does it mean I'm getting old? Soon, I'll be leaving presents to open till after lunch. I might even fall asleep before opening them. Imagine that."

Holly nudged me with her elbow. "Does anyone in your family do that?"

An image of Christmas Day with Mum, Gran and Aunt Ellen ripping open their presents one after the other and holding their favoured loot aloft came to my mind. They could hardly contain themselves till after breakfast.

I shook my head. "Not really."

"Well then."

We sat in silence for a few moments, the air stained and blurry. The smell of flattened mud and grass filled the air, the path in front of us chilled and damp. Holly wore black jeans, a green beanie and a new pair of black and gold Nikes. She'd always followed fashion way more than I did, mainly because she had the 6-foot-2 frame to pull off any item of clothing she fancied.

"You know what I really want for Christmas?" I said.

Holly sunk lower on the bench. "A minute ago, it was nothing, but do tell."

"I want a girlfriend. Last year I didn't have one, but that was okay because it was too soon after Amy. But this year is different. This year, I want to share my favourite time of year with someone special. I want to really enjoy the holidays."

I heard Holly grin — her jaw always made a noise when she did. "You want a girlfriend for Christmas?"

"I do."

"Well that's easy enough," she said.

I sat up and looked at her. "Is it?"

She nodded. "Sure. We just make you a billboard, drop you in the middle of Oxford Street and away you go."

I scowled. "I'm being serious."

She smiled. "So am I."

I stood up and paced around in front of Holly, the nearby trees creating eerie shadows. "If I had a girlfriend, she'd have to buy me something — *she'd* have to think of an amazing present, wouldn't she?"

"Which is the perfect reason to get one." Holly was being ironic, but I ignored her.

I cast my mind back to the last time I'd had a serious girlfriend. Amy. For Christmas, she'd bought me a hot-air balloon ride one year, a ski jacket the next. I wanted that this year. I wanted to receive presents not bought by my mum or gran. I wanted to go ice-skating and kiss while we held hands. I wanted drunken Christmas sex. And I wanted it all now.

"But it's November 25th — Christmas is only a month away," Holly said. She was far more practical than me. Holly favoured order and spreadsheets, so I could see how this sudden plan troubled her.

I wagged a finger in her direction, twisting one way, then the other. "It involves a deadline though, and you must admit I work well to deadlines."

Holly nodded. "You do." Then she cocked her head, holding up a single finger. "But I have one question."

"Shoot."

"Is this all because of Melanie Taylor?"

I paused, then bit the inside of my right cheek. "No." It was, but I wasn't about to admit that right away.

"So it's just coincidence we heard she's getting married this morning, you think she's an idiot, and now you want a girlfriend?"

I bristled at the suggestion, mainly because it was mostly true.

"It's not to do with her — it's just time. It's been nearly a year and a half since Amy, and I'm ready for another relationship. I'm not talking about marriage, I'm talking about getting a girlfriend. There's a big difference." I turned my head to Holly as the wind whipped my hair in my face. I swiped it left. "It would just be nice to meet someone who gets me."

"I get you," Holly said, spreading her palms.

"Is that an offer?" I asked.

Holly and I had always flirted, it was part of our make-up. But we'd been friends for 16 years now, and we both knew that flirting was as far as it was ever going to go.

Holly grinned at me. "Do you want it to be?"

I rolled my eyes and resumed my pacing. "You know what I mean. Yes, you get me, but I want a romantic partner to get me. I want someone to take me to dinner, have a conversation and laugh at my jokes. I want to be wooed."

Holly's laughter punctured the descending gloom. "Laughing at your jokes? That's a tall order."

"My jokes are legendary," I said.

"In your head," Holly replied. "That one about the stick?"

"What's brown and sticky? That's a classic."

We both laughed now.

It had been one of those crisp, sunny autumn days that I loved, the kind that made you want to snap out of your normal life, roll up the sunshine and start afresh. Sometimes in autumn, the barren trees left me feeling empty, but today, they were lining a new path, setting me off in a new direction.

Holly was silent for a moment, her nose pointing skywards, her cheeks flushed from the cold. She sat forward before speaking. "You're a romantic, Tori. Always have been, always will be. But I'll help if that's what you want." She crossed her legs in front of her. "How do you plan on scoring said perfect woman?"

I rubbed my hands together and breathed on them, even though I knew it wouldn't do any good. We needed to get inside where it was warm. "I don't know, I only just decided. But the internet seems a good place to start." I started to hop from one foot to the other.

"If you like weirdos."

"I love weirdos, you know that. I thrive on them." Of course, I hadn't really thought about exactly how I was going to snag my perfect mate — the idea had only come to me today after getting Melanie Taylor's news.

We began to walk towards the park gates, Holly towering over me. Holly's height drew stares everywhere we walked, like now. We didn't pay them any attention — we were used to it.

"Anyway," I continued. "Melanie met whatshername online."

Holly punched her hands into the pockets of her thick coat, her laughter a howling gale around us both. "You're using Melanie's relationship as a barometer of online sanity? Can I remind you Melanie is a circus freak show all on her own?"

I nudged Holly with my elbow. "She's not that bad — and she's got a girlfriend."

Holly stopped walking. "We are talking about the same Melanie, aren't we? The one who got so off her face at Alison's wedding, she puked on the groom's mum? The same Melanie who drove her car into a fence when she was on an empty road? The same Melanie who married someone and divorced them within three months?"

I let the sentence hang for a few seconds before replying. "I know all of that — but Milly says she's changed since she met this woman. Apparently, she's way calmer, a different person. And Milly said she seemed happier too — happier than she's seen her in a long time."

Holly scoffed again. "It won't last. Melanie has crazy stamped through her core. She'll find a way to fuck it up."

We were approaching the tall, black iron park gates now, the early evening sharp around us.

"I disagree. I think Melanie was just waiting for the right person and she's found her. She's been saved. I like the thought of that. I want someone to come along and sweep me off my feet, make me see the world in a different way. And if that could happen at Christmas time, I might burst with happiness."

Holly blew on to her hands before putting an arm around me. "You don't need saving — you're fine as you are."

"Maybe." I paused before continuing. "But maybe there's someone out there who can make me the best version of myself I can possibly be — there's always room for improvement, isn't there?"

Holly shrugged. "I suppose."

"Good," I said. "So starting tonight, it's Operation Christmas and you're going to be my wingwoman, just like in a terrible 80s movie." I stopped walking and turned to Holly who had an amused look on her face. "And I know you don't believe me, but I'm deadly serious." I paused. "Are you in?"

Holly stroked her rounded chin before answering. "One month is a tight deadline to meet someone and call them your girlfriend."

"I'm aware."

"But if a Christmas girlfriend is what you're after, together we'll look in every street in London to find the perfect woman. Who knows, we might even find someone for me too." Holly smiled at the thought.

"We might both find a girlfriend for Christmas," I said, my smile radiating just how happy that would make me. "Now that really would be a Hollywood movie ending." I linked my arm through Holly's as we walked on to the main road and headed back to our flat.

"But I'd like to say again," Holly added, "the current version of you doesn't need any saving. You're fine just the way you are."

I grinned up at her. "I've said it before and I'll say it again: your sweet talk will get you everywhere."

2

Saturday November 26th

To get online, the first thing I had to do was write my profile. I pulled up the app Melanie had success with, and after filling in all my details, I was asked for five key phrases to describe myself.

What would my friends say? Flighty, indecisive, tequila-intolerant, brunette, good tits. I wasn't sure I should go with that.

What about me? I pulled out a pad and pen, then began writing. Average height and build, shoulder-length maple brown hair, loves cats, tans easily. I wrinkled my nose — I needed to make it more than just another lesbian with a fondness for pussies.

Okay, take two. Five phrases or words. I could do this, I worked in marketing for goodness sake. I tapped my pen on my pad but my mind went blank. Eventually after a few minutes, I wrote: athletic, good dancer, blue eyes, deadline-driven, likes avocados. *Deadline-driven?*

Honestly, I was rubbish at this. Perhaps this was why GSOH was so popular.

I needed help. I got up and walked through to the lounge, where Holly was stretched out on the couch watching football. Holly worked as a recruitment consultant in the City, a hangover of a job from her post-university years. She had a degree in history and politics, which she'd soon realised led to precisely no jobs in the real world. So when a friend of a friend had offered her a position in his firm, she'd taken it. That had been five years ago. Now, she spent her days placing people in jobs they may or may not want and got paid handsomely for it.

I squinted at the TV. "Who's playing?" I sat on the opposite end of the sofa.

Holly didn't move her gaze from the screen. "Us and Chelsea."

I tapped my foot a few times before speaking again. "So you know my profile?"

Holly didn't respond.

"Hols?"

She ignored me again.

"Hollister?"

She looked at me. "Your profile."

"Yeah — can you help me?"

"At half-time."

"Okay." I stood up, biting my fingernail. "You want a cup of tea?"

"Please," she replied.

Our shared flat had white walls and a laminate floor, a blank canvas to decorate. However, because we were renting, we couldn't do that without our landlord's permission so we kept it minimalist. One corner of our living room held the L-shaped sofa and TV, one corner a small white dining table and chairs. The kitchen took up another corner, and we also managed to fit in a small desk. Surprisingly, the room still felt spacious.

At half-time, Holly slurped her tea while thinking of five key phrases to describe me. "How about annoying, interrupts football matches, drinks wine too fast, prone to hiccups, perky breasts?" She waited for my response.

"I predicted you'd mention my breasts."

"They're worth mentioning," Holly said. "I've always told you, I'll exchange some of my height for some of your breasts. Seems a fair swap."

I laughed. "It would be — but it's not helping to write my profile, is it? And I'm not mentioning my breasts — that seems desperate."

Holly raised an eyebrow in my direction.

"I am *not* desperate!"

Holly grinned as a train rattled by on the track just outside the window.

Our flat was in a shabby chic, up-and-coming area. South-facing, it was baking hot all year round, which meant we had the windows open constantly. It was also noisy, built right next to a train track. Hence when a train passed by, it was best to shut up until it'd passed if you wanted to be heard. We both stared at the train full of people heading into the city. Once the train was out of earshot, we refocused.

After a couple of minutes, Holly clicked her fingers together. "Got it — how about this: Christmas cracker seeks possible Mrs Claus. Must love Christmas, tinsel, ice-skating and mulled wine. Post-Christmas activities also considered on application."

"It makes me sound like I might murder them in their sleep with my special Christmas ham."

"I disagree — it's themed, it's unusual, it'll make you stand out. Plus, isn't this quest all about finding someone for Christmas, someone to spend the holiday with? You want them to love Christmas, don't you?"

I paused. "Of course, but there might be a gorgeous Muslim or Jewish lesbian out there who doesn't do Christmas. I don't want to alienate her."

Holly waved a hand through the air. "You're overthinking it. If there's a non-Christian dyke who likes the sound of you, I don't think the whole Christmas deal will put her off. Plus, Christmas is cute. It's fun, it's light, it's airy. Christmas spells romance."

Half an hour later, I was sat on my bed with my iPad, trying to work Holly's spiel into a more workable format. But the more I thought about it, the more I was inclined to agree. This would make me stand out from the crowd. People might think I was a Christmas nut who secretly wanted to be an angel or a fairy, but so be it. It was worth a shot, and if I had no bites in a few days, I could always change it. I posted the best image of me I could find, hammered out the words before I could talk myself out of it and clicked post.

Let the games commence.

***

My history as a lesbian Lothario wasn't great, truth be told — but I was determined this December was going to be different and memorable. I was tired of floating in a sea of lesbian debris. This time, I wanted to take control and steer my course with confidence.

I first kissed another woman in the school library when I was 16. Her name was Nicola Sheen and she had the smoothest skin in our class. Honestly, if Nicola walked in right now, the girlfriend search would be over because to my 16-year-old self, Nicola Sheen was the perfect woman. Tall, dark and devastatingly handsome, the fact she had a boyfriend called Craig only made me want her more. At 16, she hadn't yet realised her true vocation was to love me.

I became friends with Nicola when we were 14, quite late in my school career — Holly treated her with suspicion, seeing as she'd been by my side since the age of 11. By the time we turned 15, I wanted to spend every waking minute with Nicola, but had no idea why. Every opportunity I had, I texted Nicola and hung out with her, and we told each other our deepest, darkest secrets. She told me she had a crush on Craig Dale way before they got together. In turn, I told her I liked Ed Hartman. It was a lie, but I had to say something.

When we told each other stuff like this, Nicola favoured lying together on the bed — she'd watched too many American movies, but I wasn't complaining. Lying next to Nicola on my flowery duvet, I'd never felt so almost-content in my whole life.

We so nearly kissed a few times, but it was always her who pulled back, always her who had a freakish look in her eyes. But then, one day in the library down the history aisle, the lines blurred. When our lips locked, the klaxon that sounded in my head was loud enough to be heard in Scotland. In that moment, I knew what the invisible struggle I'd been grappling with was, and my life changed.

Nicola sunk into the kiss, even slipping her tongue into my mouth. I remember I groaned — why wouldn't I? I'd been waiting for this moment for 16 years. Most straight people have their first meaningful kiss before they reach their teenage years. Mine didn't arrive till I was old enough to get married, smoke and join the army. I'd kissed boys before, but kissing Nicola Sheen made *much* more sense. If she'd proposed right there and then, I'd have dropped everything and said yes.

But she didn't. Of course she didn't. Instead, she pulled back, looked at me with a veil of horror falling over her face and ran out of the history aisle as if I'd just produced a gun. She avoided me for days afterwards, despite my constant texting. And when she did eventually speak to me, it was to tell me we should keep our distance from each other, because what happened could never happen again.

However, such grand statements only played more into my love-struck hands. I was studying English literature after all, and this seemed to have all the hallmarks of a dramatic Shakespearian tragedy. Only, I was convinced our story would have a happy ending — the folly of youth.

Three months later, Nicola announced she was pregnant. She *really* went out of her way to tell the world she wasn't a lesbian. After that, she moved away and we lost touch. I knew she had a miscarriage and went to university, but I often wondered where she was and if she ever thought of me and that kiss. Or even if she'd ever had another kiss like that one. I knew I hadn't.

At university, I got together with a woman named Melissa. She was on the hockey team and was a real competitor at everything in life — including being the best in our relationship. She was an expert in putting me down and I was an expert at taking it, until around two years into our liaison when she decided to sleep with someone else and I was off the hook. I slept with a couple more women after that, but gave up on relationships for a while, happy to have the space to breathe.

I stayed in Bristol after graduating from its university, taking a job in a local marketing firm that set sail to my current career. The company was a small family-run business and I loved it there — I'm still in touch with them and visit every time I head west. Three months into working there, I met Amy, who owned the pet shop next door.

And after Nicola Sheen, Amy was my second significant love.

Everybody loved Amy — my mum, my friends, my colleagues — *everyone*. There really was nothing not to love. She owned her own business, loved animals and was one of the most caring people I'd ever met.

After a year, I moved into her neat three-bed terrace, the floors covered with Amy's carpets, the walls with Amy's artwork. After two years, Amy started making noises about having children — at 35, her biological clock was booming. At 24, mine was not. A year later, Amy proposed: one knee, roses, diamonds, the works. I accepted, we told the world, and the world embraced us as one.

Only I couldn't sleep. Couldn't close my eyes without thinking about getting married and having children, all before I knew what I was doing with my life. Before I was ready. I was only in my mid-20s, and suddenly, my life had been thrown into fifth gear.

After three months, Amy asked if I still wanted to get married.

I told her I didn't know.

That was enough for her.

We split up two months later amid a backdrop of tears and what-ifs. I couldn't stay in Bristol, so I handed in my notice and moved into Holly's spare room in east London.

Moving in with her was the perfect choice because Holly had known me for over half my life. She knew I loved Mexican food, garlic mayonnaise, and cats. She knew I'd still worn knee-high socks at High School far later than it was considered cool to do so. She'd held my hair when I vomited after drinking too many pints of Snake Bite on my 18th birthday. Aged 25, London and Holly were the far better option — better than being married with kids.

So yes, love. It's come my way twice, and if I'm honest, I sometimes wonder if I've used up my lot. Should I have married Amy and stayed in Bristol? I might already be a mother — I knew Amy was.

I shook my head. No, I'd done the right thing moving east. But now, 18 months later and after precisely three one-night stands and a four-date fling, I was ready to get back in the game. I wanted a girlfriend. I'd already fallen in love with city life, which took a little time for a country bumpkin like me. Now, I was ready to fall in love for real with a living, breathing woman, rather than that mannequin in Top Shop who I always think would make a fine lesbian.

Tomorrow night was date one. Her name was Ruby.

If she kissed anything like Nicola Sheen, that would be amazing.

3

Monday November 28th

I was a Cancerian and Ruby was a Scorpio. According to most experts, that meant we were a match made in lesbo-heaven. If we got together, my future was set to be awash with emotional rapport, empathy, compassion and sensitivity. One site I checked last night even said we were 'sextile', whatever that meant. One thing was certain — even before Ruby turned up, we were destined for greatness.

We'd arranged to meet in the West End, in a run-of-the-mill Soho boozer. It wasn't a gay bar, but then again, there weren't many of those left these days. Apparently with equal marriage and all the rest, we simply didn't need gay bars any more. I wasn't sure I agreed.

I loved this part of Christmas — the build-up. Don't get me wrong, I loved the day itself too, but it was the anticipation that thrilled me every year. When I was little, my parents would bring me to the West End to see the Christmas lights as an annual treat. We'd get hot chocolate, hot dogs and cinnamon donuts, and the size and sparkle of the event never failed to amaze me. Even now, years later, the sight of the West End Christmas lights still flush my insides with festive cheer. They also make me miss my dad so much, I have to stop and catch my breath.

I'd styled my shoulder-length maple hair with a new product, but it felt odd, like a dry alien life-form perched on top of my scalp. However, my foundation was smoothed in, my lipstick so bright it could stop ships. I'd done a fashion show for Holly the night before and we'd settled on some tailored black trousers and a black shirt — simple, but effective. The stage was set, now I just needed my Juliet. Or Ruby, as the case may be.

I bought myself a glass of Merlot and nabbed a table at the back of the pub. It was November 28th and already the place was overrun with Christmas spirit — by that, I mean drunk office workers. Scarves lay abandoned on the scuffed wooden floor as drinks were hoisted, ties were loosened and heels crunched on broken glass. London had come alive to celebrate the imminent birth of baby Jesus.

I recognised Ruby straight away from her profile picture — she had crazy curly hair, so she was easy to spot. She struck me as the kind of person who was always catching her breath, always rushing, always late. She just had that aura about her.

It was her love of tennis that had drawn me to her profile — that, and the fact she made a good joke about cats. I was desperate for a cat, but Holly wasn't keen — I was still working on her. If I ended up with Ruby, not only were we sextile, we'd also have cats. Perhaps three of them.

She squeezed past the crowd to sit down in the chair I pushed out for her. Ruby was carrying a pint of lager and a posh-looking laptop bag that screamed "steal me!".

She shook off her coat and smoothed herself down, before we smiled shyly at each other and shook hands. She had a strong handshake, not too firm, just right.

Ruby turned out to be in the music industry. I pricked up my ears — not only cats and perfect compatibility, but also free gig tickets on the horizon. This was getting better. She was around my age but needed a better moisturising routine — the skin around her eyes and mouth was dry and drawn — but winter could do that to you. She was wearing a floral perfume that she'd clearly just reapplied, and her pink lips were rounded and glistening with lip balm. I leaned closer to get a look at the logo that was stamped liberally around her shirt.

"Is it a squirrel?" I pointed my finger at one of the animals sitting happily on her breast. However, Ruby moved at that critical moment and my finger brushed her nipple.

She shot backwards as if I'd just slapped her.

I held up a hand as my cheeks hissed into red action. "Sorry — I was just pointing at the animal on your breast."

More blushing. "I mean, your shirt. Is it a squirrel?" This wasn't going well.

Luckily, Ruby had a sense of humour. She peered down at her shirt. "That's a funny-looking squirrel — it was a rabbit last time I looked." She gave me a grin. "So, is this a usual habit — feeling up your dates within five minutes?" She took a sip of her pint, never taking her eyes from me.

I blushed a deeper shade of red. "I normally give it at least ten."

But after that, things took a turn for the better. One thing I didn't have to worry about was flowing conversation. Ruby liked to talk. And talk and talk, which suited me as I was happy to listen, smile, nod and assess. Was Ruby going to be my future girlfriend? I was just happy that the chat was about celebrities, the best lunchtime salads, cats and tennis.

"So do you have a cat?"

Ruby shook her head. "I'd like one, but it's just not very practical. Living in a flat-share isn't the ideal environment for a couple of kittens, is it? When I get a place of my own, which will be in about 200 years at the current rate of progress with my finances, then maybe." She sighed and sat back in her chair. "Until then, I'm going to be catless and sad." She pouted to emphasise the point.

I decided Ruby was a contender — she had an easy smile and was wearing heels, which showed effort or stupidity, depending on how you looked at it. Her hair looked like it had been dipped in sunshine and she made me feel completely at ease, which was no mean feat. Perhaps the girlfriend quest would be over before December had even dawned? Perhaps Ruby was the one to tip the balance and prove that not everyone on the internet was desperate?

She seemed too good to be true. Why the hell was she still single?

***

Two hours later, I had my first clue as to just why that might be.

First, Ruby was a fan of drinking and this became obvious to me just over an hour into our date. Now don't get me wrong, I'm not a teetotal prude, far from it. However, Ruby was on to her fifth pint of lager while I was still sipping my second glass of wine. Perhaps she was nervous and deserved the benefit of the doubt? All of a sudden, that wrinkled skin around her eyes made more sense.

Second, by her fifth pint, she also told me she'd love to introduce me to Jesus Christ our Lord. A personal introduction? I was flattered.

"What are you doing on Thursday?" Ruby asked, her eyes glassy, her skin blotchy.

"Why?" Nothing that involved her, I was pretty sure.

"We've got a special 'Let Jesus Into Your Life At Christmas' evening at our church. I'd love for you to come along," she replied.

"Oh, I'm busy on Thursday," I lied, smiling.

I checked my watch. With any luck, Holly should be ringing any minute now with my get-out-of-jail phone call.

Holly forgot her emergency call.

4

Tuesday November 29th

"An extra hour of pain and an extra £7 — that's what your failed call cost me." I scowled at Holly from one end of our grey sofa. She was lying on the longer part as usual, with the TV set to the food channel. When left alone, Holly had been known to ingest three or four hours of food programming at a time. It was a habit that needed checking occasionally.

"Why £7?"

"That's how much my extra glass of wine cost me." I paused. "I should charge you."

Holly spluttered as she laughed. "You could try, but I don't think you'd get very far."

I sighed and spread my palms upwards. "I'm just not sure this internet dating game is for me. I mean, how can things go so wrong? On paper, she was perfect." I sighed. "We're on to day four now, it's nearly December. I don't have time to waste."

"You're being unrealistic. This was your first date. The next one is bound to be better. I mean, it really has to be judging by what you just told me." Holly was eating a packet of pickled onion Monster Munch and the smell was seeping into every square inch of the living room.

"I know," I said. "But it was a pretty inauspicious start." I frowned my best frown.

"It could have been worse — at least she was pretty." Holly licked her fingers of Monster Munch debris. "And she liked a bit of Jesus, so what? You like Barry Manilow, everybody has their vices." She gave me a wide grin. "Anyhow, date number two is a goer. I can feel it in my bones. What's her name again?"

"Anna," I replied.

Holly gave a curt nod. "She sounds reliable. Anna won't let you down. She'll laugh at your jokes, I guarantee it."

I didn't look so sure. "I dunno — she sounds like a librarian."

Holly scrunched up her face. "And what's wrong with librarians? Without them, the world would be in chaos. In my experience, librarians are cool, calm and collected. And they know where you left your keys."

"She's not *actually* a librarian. She does something in the City."

Holly yawned, mouth wide open, arms stretched above her head. "Even better. Ordered and rich. She can sort your spreadsheets out. And if this one fails, just remember, you've got me to come home to. What could be better?"

I gave her a wide smile. "Just don't forget the phone call this time, okay?"

"That's the spirit," Holly replied.

5

Thursday December 1st

I was sitting in the staff lounge when my phone went — it was my mum. I turned down the radio, which was blaring out 'Do They Know It's Christmas', the original Band Aid version.

"Hey kiddo." It was my mum's standard greeting. "Just calling to make sure your December plans are in place."

I smiled a sad smile — Mum did this call every year now. It used to be the province of my dad, the original Christmas enthusiast and the person who had pumped the festive season into an unmissable yearly excitement-fest for me.

Unfortunately, he'd also died on the same day seven years earlier, a few months after my 20th birthday. An untimely heart attack on his second favourite day of the year, December 1st. Despite that though, Mum had carried on their traditions without missing a beat, even though I know how hard that must have been for her. And now, here she was, keeping the spirit alive.

"All good — I'll be putting up the tree and the decorations later, like always," I said.

"Did you get the Advent calendar?"

I swallowed down some tears that threatened. Even seven years on, they could take me by surprise. "I did, thanks. It arrived yesterday."

Dad always bought us all individual calendars for the festive season, and this was another tradition that had continued even when I'd left home. Dad said he'd do it until I was married, then my wife could take over. For now, it was still Mum calling the Advent calendar shots.

"I got you a chocolate one — got myself a picture one, though. You're still young enough, I've got to watch my waistline."

I blinked as I pictured my dad with his chocolate calendar. He was always up first and he'd always eaten his chocolate before anyone else, like a naughty schoolboy. I always assumed he'd been hard done by as a child, but apparently not — he just loved Christmas and chocolate.

"How you doing?" My voice was shaky, but I knew Mum would understand.

"I'm okay," she replied. "Some days are better than others." A pause. "But I still love Christmas, still love all the memories we made over the years." She rallied. "I bought your gran a calendar too. She told me I was mad, but I think she was secretly pleased."

I chuckled down the phone. "Like every year?"

"Pretty much." She paused. "So what's new with you — job okay?"

I nodded, even though I knew she couldn't see me. "Yep, all fine. Job's good, and I'm on a dating marathon to find a girlfriend by Christmas. It's not going too well so far."

I could hear Mum frown down the phone.

"Stop frowning," I said.

"How do you know I'm frowning?"

"I just do."

A pause. "A dating marathon? Those two words don't sound like they go together."

"You might be right, but I'll let you know after date two, which is tonight."

Another pause — I could tell Mum wasn't behind this plan. "Why the sudden rush to get a girlfriend?"

"I just thought it was time, you know." I let the sentence hang, and so did my mum.

"And what does Holly have to say about this?" she asked eventually.

"About the same as you — she thinks I'm being ridiculous."

My mum's soft laugh landed in my ear. "Well, tell her hi from me, and tell her she's welcome at Christmas too."

"I will," I said. "Listen, I have to go. Thanks for the calendar. I'll call you tomorrow."

"Okay, but just be careful," Mum replied. "You're my

only daughter and I worry about your heart. Listen to what Holly says, I trust her."

"More than you trust me?" There was a slight hint of indignation in my voice.

"Sometimes, yes."

6

Friday December 2nd

I worked for an online marketing company in central London, and I loved the buzz of working in the capital. Based in a team of 30, I was a solid performer, a big fish in a small pond. The owner, Sal, trusted my judgement, there was a fantastic coffee machine and free pastries daily. It's amazing what such small stuff can do for staff morale.

I was sitting at the staff room table, working out some figures for a quote when Sal walked in. Sal used to have long, flowing red hair, but last year she'd been diagnosed with cancer and had lost it all to chemo. Now, she wore it short and it really suited her. She was also mistaken for a lesbian far more these days, but told me she quite enjoyed the added attention.

"Morning, No. 1 Lesbian." That's what she called me. Honestly, without any prompting. "How's the dating game?" Sal made herself an espresso, then came and sat opposite me at the table.

"Painful." I turned down both sides of my mouth in a comedy frown.

"Oh dear, what happened?"

"Let's see," I said, counting on my fingers. "Date one was with a drunk Christian, and date two was with an uptight banker who called time on our date after a single coffee — like I'm the worst catch of the century."

"Ouch," Sal said. "Some people just don't know when they strike it lucky. What was her problem?"

I shrugged. "No idea, but Anna did not like what she saw when confronted with me, so she bailed sharpish. Holly was so sure it would work too. I couldn't sleep last night thinking about it — am I that bad she had to run when the froth on her flat white was still warm?"

"And there was me going to start moaning about my life. Sounds like you need a coffee."

"So long as it's not a flat white," I said, laughing despite myself. "But let's see what date three brings tonight."

"Tonight? You're packing them in."

I laughed. "That's what Holly said. She reminded me I had a duty to go out with her too. So we're doing that tomorrow — a date-free Saturday."

"Good. I don't want you turning into one of those serial daters who struggle to cope with the real world." Sal took a sip of her coffee and sighed. She looked tired, but that's what having two-year-old twins will do.

"I promise I'll get out before I turn too weird." I paused. "Besides, I can't do this for a prolonged period of time. I think my body might have a breakdown and I know my wallet would. Dating is an expensive pastime and I'm already exhausted. Can't you see the amount of make-up I'm wearing today?" I circled my face and jutted out my chin.

"You'll get no sympathy here with tales of sleep woe. Sleep is something I fondly remember, like something from another, simpler life. Only my lack of sleep is due to two little rascals, rather than burning the candle at both ends." A smile crossed Sal's face as she spoke about her daughters. Then she leaned over the table and fixed me with her gaze. "But the question is, have you had a snog out of it yet?"

I gave her a rueful smile. "Not last night, she bailed before I'd finished stirring my drink. And Ruby? Well, she tried to kiss me as we left, but she only got my cheek. Nothing passionate."

"But tonight could be the passionate one?"

I shrugged. "We'll see. She might be a raving lunatic or she might be the woman of my dreams."

Sal laughed. "What's her name?"

"Sienna," I replied.

Sal gave a slow nod. "Sienna — sounds like a bit of posh totty to me." She smiled, before raising her espresso cup. "Here's to you and Sienna — may you have a night filled with passionate kisses."

I clinked my imaginary coffee cup to hers.

***

December 2nd and I was already on date three — even I was impressed at the speed of my progress. Holly had already told me I had to be more choosy, but being choosy was what had got me here in the first place.

I was still exhausted, as today had been a busy day with three external meetings. I'd tramped across half of London, and my face felt like it needed to be put on a hot wash after miles of Tube travel. About the last thing I wanted to do right now was go on a date. My ideal date for tonight would be my duvet and my bed.

I headed to the Thai restaurant where I was meeting Sienna, which was decorated in suitably chintzy shades of gold and pink. I'd wanted to try out this restaurant for a while now as it'd been getting stellar reviews. Tonight it was packed with customers all chowing down on Thai classics with a modern twist, and the scent of coriander, garlic and chilli made my mouth water. I spruced up my make-up in the toilets before taking a seat.

Sienna worked in the charity sector, which immediately put her on the moral high ground. She was from East London, had a cockney accent that curled at the edges and a definite orange hue. She arrived half an hour late which didn't endear her to me, causing me to drink a glass of wine before she arrived. Couple that with my extreme tiredness and I could feel my eyelids getting heavy before she sat down.

"Sorry I'm late, I got stuck at work." A waft of cigarette smoke sailed across my nostrils as she unwound her massive rainbow scarf and sat down, eagerly perusing the menu. "Have you ordered already?"

"Only a glass of wine while I waited." I indicated my empty glass.

"Fab — I'll get a bottle. Was it red?"

I nodded and she got the attention of a nearby waiter.

So, Sienna looked like her profile picture — tick. After all the scary stories I'd heard about online dating, I half-expected one of my dates to turn up and be a man. However, Sienna was very much a woman, her low-cut top providing an invitation to her breasts — double tick. She had short, black hair and was dressed casually in trousers and a red top. She was promising.

"So sorry about my time-keeping again. Our American office decided they wanted to chat just as I was walking out the door." She threw me an apologetic smile as she shifted in her seat to get comfortable.

"American office? Sounds like you're in banking and not the charity sector."

She shook her head. "A lot of people think that — but the charity sector is a big, global business these days. We're always on the lookout for donations and ways to spend the money best. Nobody sleeps, believe me."

Mention of sleep deprivation made me open my eyes wider. I wanted to appear as alert as possible, even though I was *this* close to slumping on the table.

The wine arrived a few minutes later and we ordered our food, then settled back to get to know each other.

It turned out that Sienna was born and raised in London and her parents still lived within a ten-minute walk of her front door.

"Really? I don't think I've ever met anyone who didn't move *to* London. I can't imagine being raised here." I shook my head. "That means you've been riding the Tube your whole life."

Sienna laughed. "I have. I used to take the Tube into town with my mates at the weekend and cause havoc. Still do, but I'm an adult now, so it's overlooked."

I grinned at her. "Funny how that works, isn't it?"

"How about you? I can't detect an accent."

I shook my head. "Oxford, no accent required. My mum's a professor there."

"Does that mean you're posh?" Sienna poured wine into my glass with a reassuring glug.

"People tend to think so, but no, it doesn't just rub off like gold dust. Besides, being a professor is a grand title with poor pay. At least, that's what my mum always tells me when I try to tap her up for a loan."

We chatted for another half an hour with no sign of food. With another glass of wine in my empty stomach, I kept having to shake my head to snap myself awake. Falling asleep at the table was definitely bad manners, but I desperately needed some food to sustain me.

A few minutes later, I excused myself to go to the loo — all the liquid had taken its toll. I sat down, sighing with tiredness, closed my eyes and leaned my head on the cool, white tiles of the toilet stall. Against my hot, red cheek they were wonderfully soothing.

Date number three wasn't going so bad. First, she'd ordered a bottle of wine which meant she had no intention of running away any time soon. Second, she hadn't tried to convert me to Jesus yet. What's more, she was attractive and seemed on my wavelength. This could be the start of something, so perhaps Sienna would be my Christmas girlfriend? Plus, Sienna was a beautiful name — I could well get used to going out with a Sienna.

I let my mind drift off as I rested my head heavier against the reassuring toilet wall. Perhaps we'd kiss outside the restaurant later, then go on to a bar and sit closer than necessary to each other. Then perhaps we'd brush each other's hands under the table. Kiss at the bus stop on the way home and send each other soppy messages tomorrow as we made plans for our second date and beyond. Perhaps…

However, when I woke up 35 minutes later, those were not the thoughts I was thinking. On opening my eyes, I squinted into the bright light of the cubicle, clutched the toilet seat and steadied myself. I peeled my head off the wall, wincing as my neck screeched at me for leaving it at such an awkward angle for over half an hour.

Where the hell was I? I rolled my shoulder and tried to loosen my upper body, which was stiff from lack of movement. I winced at the pain, while wiping up dribble from my chin and my shoulder with some toilet tissue.

I clung on to the toilet roll dispenser while my brain tried to make sense of the situation. Why was I asleep on a toilet? A toilet that wasn't even mine? And since when did I fall asleep on toilets?

And then it came to me.

I was on a date. I was on a *ruddy date*.

But instead of sitting opposite my date, being charming and laughing at all of her jokes, I was dribbling on a toilet with my trousers around my ankles.

I closed my eyes and exhaled. I was the world's worst date, in widescreen technicolour. With a cherry on the top.

And it had all been going *so* well.

The last thing I wanted to do right now was get up off the toilet and face my mistake. But it was the one thing I had to do, especially if I wanted the kissing, drinking and soppy text messages to take place. All of which had seemed a pretty sure bet 40 minutes ago. But now? Not so much.

I rubbed the heels of my hands into my eyes to wake myself up, then swore lightly under my breath as I remembered too late I'd applied extra mascara before the date. I was now pretty sure that extra mascara was smeared down my cheeks. I wiped dribble from my mouth again and got myself upright, pulling up my trousers and crashing into the toilet wall as I did. I stopped and steadied myself again, breathing deeply through a blurred haze. My head was foggy, like I was shipwrecked.

I hurled myself out of the stall, staggering left, then

right. I slowed my movements, allowing my body a chance to wake up — it was clearly still asleep and who could blame it? I clutched the sink in front of me, and sure enough, when I surveyed my face, I looked like a drunk, mascara-obsessed panda. Triffic.

I splashed some water on my face and frantically tried to use some tissue to clean it up, but I only managed to smear the mascara over a wider area. I shook my head and laughed at my reflection, mild hysteria swelling inside. If Sienna hadn't already left, she was certain to run like the wind when she saw the horror story walking towards her.

I straightened my hair the best I could, already composing my apologies in my head. But what exactly did you say to someone when you'd left them sitting alone for over half an hour? Did you admit to falling asleep, or make up some emergency? I decided to go with the emergency option.

I drew myself up to my full height, pulling my shoulders back as my mother always told me to. Then I pushed open the door and strode back into the restaurant with as much swagger as I could muster, only to be greeted by an empty table and a half-drunk glass of wine. I spun my gaze around the room but I had to face facts — Sienna had gone and I can't say I blamed her.

I sat down and exhaled, before getting the waiter's attention as my stomach rumbled.

"The other woman — has she left?"

The waiter gave me a sad smile and a nod. "She go,"

he said, turning his head towards the door. "And she cancel your food too."

Shit. This was not going to be good for my dating reputation. I put my head in my hands as my stomach rumbled again. Then I reached into my bag and grabbed my phone, pulling up Sienna's number. I paused, my fingers hovering over the keys. Now I had the phone in my hand, what exactly was I supposed to say? 'So sorry, I fell asleep in the toilet'? Try as I might, I couldn't come up with a better plan. I decided to sleep on it.

I put my phone on the table and glanced at my watch: just gone 9pm. There was still wine left, and I'd wanted to try this restaurant for a while now. Plus, I was starving as my stomach kept reminding me. I needed something to soak up the alcohol.

I signalled to the waiter again.

"Could I still get some food?"

He nodded.

I consulted the menu again, ordered and sat back. At least if the food was as good as the reviews, this night wouldn't turn out to be a total disaster. Best to look on the bright side.

Just then, 'Last Christmas' by Wham! began to flow from the restaurant speakers, presumably to rub salt in my wounds. I had nobody special to give my heart to. I was a sad, sleepy loser.

I poured Sienna's wine into my glass and saw someone waving out of the corner of my eye. I turned to my left.

It was Melanie Taylor, a smile breaking out on her face as she saw me. She was sitting with what I could only assume was her new fiancée, just two tables along from me.

Oh no, not now. Not when I looked like a starved raccoon.

Before I could react, Melanie was on the move, reaching my table in seconds. Her closely cropped hair was sitting just-so on her head, and I wasn't sure her smile could get any wider. Clearly, Melanie was loved up.

"How *are* you?" Melanie already had her arms wide open, and her smile had changed to a concerned, pitiful expression that said 'eating out alone again?' I wanted to sink under the table. On top of everything, I didn't need Melanie Taylor to rub her happiness in my face. However, I was out of luck.

"I want you to meet my fiancée!" Melanie turned and beckoned her over with rapid hand movements. I heard a chair scrape back as I braced myself to be nice — after all, it wasn't Melanie's fault that love was shining on her, but not me.

Within seconds, her new partner was standing beside her, giving me an awkward smile. Melanie Taylor had landed on her feet and no mistake. But hang on, there was something ever-so-familiar about her partner — a smile I knew, piercing almond eyes that I'd looked into before. It couldn't be, could it?

But before my sleepy brain could piece the puzzle

together, Melanie had her arm around her girlfriend's shoulders, her face radiating so much happiness, I felt the heat. However, my whole body heated up for a totally different reason now her girlfriend was up close and personal.

I did know those eyes, that mouth.

And from the narrowing of her eyes, she recognised me too.

"Tori, I want you to meet Nic, my fiancée. Nic, this is Tori."

We both stared at each other and nobody said a word.

I could see Melanie was confused, and rightly so. She'd just introduced her fiancée to one of her friends, and now neither was saying a word to the other. However, if she'd peered inside my head at that moment, she would have seen a ticker-tape parade reading 'OMG! OMG! OMG!' circling round my brain.

Nicola Sheen, my first love, had just shown up at my table and she was engaged to my crazy friend. I heard the crescendo in my ears as my heart sank to the floor, sobbing uncontrollably. I wanted to stand up and shake Nicola, ask her what the hell she was doing here after all these years. And engaged to *someone else*.

But I didn't. I just sat and stared. Externally, I was quiet. Inside, I was exploding like a gamma-ray.

After what seemed like an eternity, Nicola put out her hand. "Victoria *Hammond*?" Her flushed face told me she couldn't believe she was asking.

Truth be told, I couldn't either. I'd been waiting to hear those words and touch this skin again for over ten years. And now, here she was. I wanted to get up and embrace Nicola, feel her against me after all this time. But I knew that wasn't social etiquette, so I stayed seated.

"Nicola." I shook my head. "All this time, and now you're Melanie's fiancée. I can't believe it!" I didn't mean that quite the way it came out.

Or perhaps I did.

Seeing her was just such a shock.

When she touched me, it took me right back — right back to the library, my bedroom, my heartbreak.

She nodded, still holding my hand. "Bit of a whirlwind, but yes, engaged." She glanced up at Melanie, before refocusing on me.

Her gaze burnt into me, and I had to remember to breathe. Nicola looked older, of course she did. Her hair was shorter, her features fuller, her body more solid. But she was still Nicola Sheen, she still owned those eyes and she still commanded that my eyes couldn't look away.

And of course, she had to meet me just after my failed date when I was looking like *this*. Thanks a bunch, universe.

I stared at her hand, then at Melanie's. There were no rings.

"Haven't got around to it yet," Melanie said as if reading my mind. "Rings are next on the list, aren't they, sweetheart?" She was gripping Nicola's shoulder harder now as if she was trying to stop the situation slipping out of her control. Melanie had brought Nicola over here to gloat. Now it turned out, she was reintroducing me to my first love and I was pretty sure that vibe was seeping out of every single pore of my body.

"I take it you two know each other?" Melanie looked from Nicola to me, then back. Her voice was too high. It scratched my skin.

I nodded. "Went to school together. Best friends for a time, weren't we?" I locked eyes with Nicola. My stomach dropped. Best friends, first kiss, could-have-been lovers. All I knew was the story we'd written at school had never been fully erased, nor fully written.

"We were, but it feels like a different life," Nicola said. And then she had the good grace to look away.

A wave of nausea hit me as Melanie kissed Nicola on the cheek — it was as if I'd just been slapped. I didn't even want to think about them having sex.

I shut my eyes, and when I reopened them, Melanie had her concerned face on again. "You know, you're welcome to come and eat with us if you're eating on your own." She looked like she wanted to take a jar of pity and smother it all over me.

I glanced at Nicola, whose face didn't alter, but I could spy alarm in her eyes — it was a look I was used to seeing when it came to her. Did Melanie know the signs yet? I doubted it.

I shook my head. "That's kind, but I'm just popping in on the way to meeting someone, so I won't be long."

It was gone 9pm, so I was clearly lying. I smiled up at Melanie. Could she tell I'd rather stick pins in my eyes than have dinner with them?

If she did, she said nothing. Instead, they walked back to their table with a promise to meet for drinks soon, Nicola Sheen avoiding my gaze.

I couldn't wait.

I took a slug of wine, refilled my glass to the top and hoped my food arrived soon. I was desperate to turn my head and get a good look at Nicola, but I knew I couldn't.

Nicola Bloody Sheen. Engaged to Melanie Bloody Taylor.

Holly was not going to believe this, and truth be told, neither did I.

I hadn't planned on getting drunk tonight, but now there seemed no other option. I downed my wine in a few gulps and ordered another large glass of red from the waiter. I didn't care how I looked anymore or what else could happen tonight — the roof of my world was already sagging to the point of near collapse. I'd been deserted on a date, fallen asleep with my trousers down and had just bumped into my first love, who was engaged to my friend. Isn't it ironic?

I made a mental note to call Alanis Morissette and see what she thought.

7

Saturday December 3rd

Holly had to stop walking, she was laughing so much. "You didn't?"

I nodded. "I did. I woke myself up dribbling." I smirked. "And it's not funny, by the way."

Holly's laughter begged to differ. "It's kinda funny, you have to admit. You go on a date and fall asleep in the toilet? That is the stuff of legend." She snorted. "I did tell you to slow down with these dates, but I thought you could take three in a week. Clearly I was wrong."

We were walking around our local park, and it was another beautifully sunny day. To our right, barren trees lined the path ahead. To our left, a group of carol singers were belting out 'Jingle Bells' with gusto. I dropped a pound coin into their collecting bucket as we passed and it hit the bottom with a thud.

"You were. Perhaps I'm developing narcolepsy like in that film. Whatever it is, this is going to seriously dent my lesbian kerb appeal." I kicked a stone and it hit a nearby tree.

Holly chuckled, her grey woollen bobble-hat waggling as she walked. "It's not ideal."

I pouted at her and sighed. "We're into December now and the girlfriend quest isn't improving, is it? Ruby was a dud, Anna couldn't leave me quick enough, then on the third... well, you know the rest."

Holly put an arm around me and squeezed. "You're being impatient, you just need to relax and give it time. Romance doesn't just knock on your door — that only happens in those films you love. Romance, like anything worthwhile, takes time and you need to give it space to breathe. You might bump into Sienna again and you'll live happily ever after. You just never know."

I raised an eyebrow in Holly's direction.

She smiled. "Long shot, but it might happen." She paused, looking away. "Or you might get together with someone you never even thought of. Someone on your doorstep, or someone who's just about to walk into your life."

I sat down on a park bench dedicated to a man called Fred — his plaque said he'd loved sitting there, and I could see the appeal. From this bench, the views of the surrounding area were laid out as far as the eye could see.

"Funny you should say that — there's more," I told Holly as she sat down next to me.

"What?"

"Last night," I began. "After Sienna left, I was still hungry. So I ordered some food." I paused. "And bear in mind, this is just after I've woken up with my trousers down and just after I've smeared mascara across my face to look like a crazy raccoon lady."

"Good image," Holly replied, snorting.

I put my head in my hands just thinking about it, then started to laugh. "Yeah so, I'm sitting there looking gorgeous. Then just before my food arrives, guess who walks up to my table when I'm sitting there like a loser, dining alone?"

"Who?"

"Melanie Taylor."

I had Holly's interest now. She spread her hands on her jeans before twisting her body to me. "Was she with her new woman?"

"She was," I said. "And we know her."

Now it was Holly's turn to look surprised. "We do? Who is it?"

"Someone you'll never guess in a million years."

A few seconds went by.

"Why aren't you guessing?"

"You just told me it was pointless, so why would I try?" she said.

Fair point. I took a deep breath. "Melanie Taylor is engaged to Nicola Sheen."

Holly's brow furrowed as she took in the news and began to process it. Her face went from disbelief to horror to comedy in a matter of seconds, but then she saw I wasn't laughing and tempered her reaction. Holly, of all people, knew my feelings on Nicola Sheen.

"Hang on," she said, circling her finger as if she was dialling back time. "Nicola Sheen is a *lesbian*?" Her voice rose at the end of her sentence.

"Apparently, yes."

Holly let out a low whistle. "Holy shit. And I bet Melanie Taylor has no idea that you were the woman who started her on the road to the promised land of lesbianville. You were the magnet who drew her in—"

"—and I was the one she fucked over for Craig Dale. *She* might not know, but I do." I shook my head, still swallowing down disbelief. "Can you believe it? Of all the women in the whole world, Melanie Taylor has to go and meet her. *Online*. This has been my dream for over ten years. How come it didn't happen to me?"

"Because you weren't registered on the app?"

I shot Holly a look. "It's ridiculous. She's known her for two months and they're *getting married*." My cheeks had flushed crimson and I could tell my ear lobes were following suit. "How can it be that Melanie Taylor has stolen my first love and is now going to be living the life I was meant to be living?"

A shard of Holly's laughter pierced the air. "Your life? Slight over-reaction perhaps?" Holly peered down at me. "And what happened to being happy for Melanie, seeing her turn over a new leaf and find happiness?"

"That was before that happiness was attached to Nicola Sheen," I replied.

We both stared out into the milky December sunshine. Nearby, a small child tottered, then fell over, but no crying ensued — he just got up and carried on with the aid of his mum.

"What did she say when she saw you?" Holly crossed her right leg over her left and concentrated on my answer.

"Neither of us said much. I mean, all these years, wondering where she was and whether or not that kiss had meant anything. And now she shows up in London and she's a *lesbian*."

"She didn't mention the panda eyes?" Holly was grinning now, barely able to contain herself.

"Let's assume she was overwhelmed with my beauty," I said, smiling despite myself.

Holly's mouth twitched. "And what did she look like, more importantly? Ten years can do things to people. I don't look much like the tall girl with the flowing hair anymore."

I stretched my neck backwards and exhaled. "She looked like Nicola," I said before glancing sideways. "Close up, I would know those eyes and that mouth anywhere. She was a bit more filled out, but not fat, and her hair was about the same length, but styled — very chic. But she's still very much Nicola Sheen."

"Soon to be Nicola Sheen-Taylor or vice versa."

I sat forward and put my head in my hands, shaking my head as I did.

"There's nothing you can do about this, you know that, right? Yes, you once kissed Nicola Sheen and ever since you have put her on a pedestal. But she exists in a bubble, in a snapshot of time. You kissed Nicola once when you were 16, and she's still the benchmark of first kisses. But here's a newsflash — you don't know Nicola Sheen. She dumped you like a hot potato after you kissed, and then she got pregnant, which was a huge over-reaction if you don't mind me saying."

I sat back up and glanced sideways at Holly. "But she was my first love."

Holly nodded. "I know — we all had one. That doesn't mean when we meet them later on in life, they're still our destiny. Everybody needs a first love, it's a marker. But then that's done — it's a first love, you move on and you meet someone new." Holly paused, clearly waiting to see if I was listening.

I was.

She carried on. "Nicola's done that — she's come out and she's met someone new. And now it's time for you to do that too. Nicola Sheen might not have given you another thought after your kiss. You might have been just one in a long line of kisses, leading up to her first girlfriend. Don't assume she's hankered after you for the past ten years in the same way that you have her."

Holly's face had turned stern now — she was flushed from her speech and her eyes were watery. I never knew Holly felt like this about my Nicola Sheen obsession.

I was somewhat startled, and a bit hurt. Way to kick a girl when she's down.

I glanced at her nervously before replying. "I know all that. I know she's probably not given me another thought, and now probably won't again after seeing me in such a state. But then again, we were each other's first female kiss—"

"How do you know that?" Holly threw her hands up in the air as she spoke. "That's your presumption, but you don't know for sure." She paused. "What would you say if I told you I snogged Nicola Sheen?"

My mouth fell open. "You didn't?" My words came out in a whisper.

Holly began to laugh. "No, I didn't. But I might have. You may or may not have been her first kiss. But even if I had, it was over ten years ago!" Holly shook her head. "You're ridiculous sometimes, you know that?"

I licked my lips and stared at her. "Why are you getting so wound up about this?"

"Because I have to live with your crazy obsessions and then I have to pick up the pieces when things don't work out as you've planned them in your mind. It's always me, Tori. Always." She ran a hand through her hair and stretched her legs out front. "Plus, I want you to be happy and I don't want to see you hurt. And that will not happen if you run after Nicola Sheen like a lovesick puppy. At best, she'll declare undying love and call off her wedding — and that would be awkward. At worst, she'll stare at you oddly and walk away, and then you'll examine what you did wrong for the next year. I would like to stop this pattern of behaviour. I'm suggesting you don't follow your heart blindly up a dead end and perhaps think about things before you act. Okay?"

I considered Holly's words as the air sagged in front of me, now silent save for the carol singers across the slab of grass who were singing 'Once In Royal David's City'. I could hear my heartbeat in my ears, elevated after Holly's outburst. When did I start to annoy her so much? As far as I was aware, we got on great, although the obsessive trait had been brought up before not just by Holly, but also by my mum and other friends. So maybe she had a point.

I put out a hand in Holly's direction and gave her a weak smile. "I won't do anything stupid, I promise," I said.

She raised an eyebrow. "Really?"

"Yes — I'm going to be adult about this. We'll go to Melanie and Nicola's wedding, and I'll clap and cheer in all the right places. I won't return to being 16 again." I pursed my lips to underline my intention.

Holly's shoulders slumped and she exhaled. "Okay, that's good to know." Then she put her arm around me and I leaned into her. "No stalking Melanie and Nicola on social media either."

I nodded my head firmly. "I promise."

But even I knew I was lying.

8

Monday December 5th

The following Monday arrived and I had no dates set up for this week. Holly had dragged me out around town on Saturday and had banned the topic of Melanie Taylor and Nicola Sheen from our vocabulary, which had been quite a trial. It was a good job she couldn't read my thoughts.

However, being busy meant I had no time to obsess, and we'd even managed to have a fun night out on the scene, slugging back far too much mulled wine as we got into the Christmas spirit. Hence yesterday had been taken up with lying on the sofa, eating crisps and watching re-runs of *Orange Is The New Black*.

Also, yesterday I'd only spent around an hour checking Melanie Taylor's Facebook account to see pictures of her with Nicola. Two months' worth of photos, it turned out. Melanie and Nicola on a river boat on the Thames, having a sunset dinner, posing in front of phone boxes.

There was even one of them kissing in the street, both wearing thick coats, eyes closed. They looked like they were in love. I cursed myself for unfollowing Melanie months earlier when her updates had got too annoying.

Today I came into work early, fired up and ready to take on the week — but my first port of call was a cup of coffee.

Sal walked in just as I'd finished grinding beans and gave me a grin. "Morning, No. 1 Lesbian — good weekend?"

I nodded. "It was okay."

She put a hand on her hip. "And how was Serena?"

"Sienna," I corrected, slotting the ground coffee into the machine and pressing the button.

Sal clicked her fingers together. "Right, Sienna." She paused and cocked her head. "But I'm guessing from the look on your face, it didn't go as well as you might have hoped."

I laughed. "It didn't — but that's not Sienna's fault. It's mine. I fell asleep halfway through the date. On the loo." I held Sal's gaze as the words sunk in.

She took a moment to reply. "How do you fall asleep on the loo?" she finally asked, grabbing a cup from the cupboard and starting on her own coffee as mine came to an end.

I waved my hand to bat the comment away. "It's a long story, and one I have consigned to the part of my brain marked 'Dumb things I have done in my time on Earth, folder two'."

Sal smirked. "Folder two? You're planning on a collection?"

"Judging from the first 27 years, I'd say it was highly likely."

I grabbed some bread from the communal bag and slotted them into the toaster, just as I heard my phone go in the office. My eyes widened. "Gotta grab this, expecting a call," I told Sal, picking up my coffee and brushing past her at speed.

"That's what I like to see, eager staff!" Sal called after me.

I got to my desk and banged down my coffee, just getting to the call before it rang off. I needn't have run, though — it wasn't the client I was expecting, it was Holly.

"Hey," I said into my phone. "You missing me already? We only saw each other an hour ago."

"Ha ha," she replied. "Just calling to remind you about those tickets."

"Tickets?" I searched my mind for what she might be referring to.

"For the Dixie Chicks gig? You said you were going to get them, remember? Anyway, they go on sale today at 10am, and I'm not going to be anywhere near a computer, so don't forget. This is your one-hour warning call."

I nodded. "Dixie Chicks, goddit."

And that's when I noticed the burning smell, right before the building's fire alarm started screeching in my ear.

"What's that noise?" Holly asked.

"Who left this toast unattended?" asked Maureen, our office manager. She folded her arms in the kitchen doorway and scoured the office looking for the culprit.

Bugger. "I gotta go," I told Holly. "I think I just set the office on fire."

I hit the red button on my phone and made my way sheepishly to the kitchen to fess up to Maureen. She already had the offending, blackened toast on the kitchen counter and was just putting on her high-vis fire warden jacket as I arrived. No matter what Maureen claimed, I think she secretly took pleasure in such episodes — any excuse to don the high-vis and have her authority ratcheted to the next level. If Maureen hadn't been a prefect at school, they'd missed a trick.

"Sorry — it was me. I got a phone call and rushed to take it." I bit my lip and gave Maureen my best 'sorry' face.

In return, she gave me a withering look — Maureen and I tolerated each other, rather than took pleasure in each other's existence. Her look told me this was no more than she expected.

"Tell that to the fire team when they turn up on a wild goose chase," she said, tutting. She rolled her eyes for good measure, then pushed past me and began shouting at the office to pack up and get out.

I made my way back into the scrum, grabbed my coffee, bag and coat, then joined the throng now exiting the office via the stairs. It wasn't just our office either — it was the whole building. A slight pang of guilt zapped through me, but then I was standing on the cold winter pavement outside our building, chatting to our finance team about their weekend. Fire alarms weren't unusual in our building, so most people took them in their stride. If there ever was an *actual* fire, it would be a shock to the system.

Ten minutes later, the giant red fire engines skidded round the corner, bringing the central London traffic to a halt. There were two of them, which seemed overkill for two pieces of toast. However, as our purchase ledger whizz Simon pointed out, they didn't know that — they just thought a building was on fire.

I winced as he said it.

The trucks parked up and a bunch of burly-looking firefighters jumped down from their trucks, their over-sized gear looking out of place on a normal city street. They walked towards Maureen who was practising her best official face, and then to my horror, she pointed towards me, before beckoning me over. I put my head down and crimson embarrassment leaked into my cheeks as I came face to face with no less than four firefighters, three men and one... Nicola Sheen. I blinked rapidly, my heartbeat thudding in my chest.

Not even in my wildest dreams had Nicola Sheen been a lesbian *and* a firefighter.

"This is the culprit," Maureen told them, her pudgy

finger pointed in my direction as if she was about to send me to the Tower for treason.

I smiled at the group. "Sorry — I usually watch my toast like a hawk," I lied.

"Try to do so in future," said Nicola, all business-like, as if attending a fire caused by your ex was an everyday occurrence. "Toasters account for a large amount of our call-outs, which is a lot of wasted time."

I nodded and furrowed my brow.

Nicola still wasn't smiling.

"Will do," I said.

"We'll go inside to do our check, then you can go back in," said the tallest of the male firefighters, nodding towards one of his colleagues who followed him in. Maureen began chatting to the other man, which left me and Nicola standing in the sharp December cold, wind needling my face as I tried to remain calm.

"We really must stop meeting like this," I said.

Finally, a semblance of a smile on Nicola's red lips. "We really must. Ten years of nothing, and then twice in a couple of days." She paused. "But then, you always did know how to make an impact on people, didn't you?"

I gulped down air, probably looking like a manic seagull. Nicola Sheen had just told me I'd made an impact on her.

Shut the front door.

"You never said you were a firefighter when I saw you the other night." I rubbed my hands together in a bid to keep them busy.

"We didn't really swap much more than pleasantries, did we? I think Melanie was just freaked out we knew each other." Nicola's fire helmet was pulled down, nearly obscuring her eyes, but I could see they were watching me closely. "She wasn't the only one who was surprised, though — you were the last person I expected to bump into."

"I hope it was a pleasant surprise." My tone was light, not giving away the fact I so desperately wanted her to be pleased. *Please be pleased.*

"Of course." She was rubbing her thumb and index finger together nervously. "It was lovely to see you. A shock, but lovely."

There was silence for a few moments as we assessed each other. Up close and without Melanie's prying glare, I could study Nicola's face properly — and she still held a certain something. Sure, she looked older, but age sat well with her — she seemed comfortable in her own skin. What's more, she still possessed deep, knowing eyes and full, rounded lips. Yep, those lips were still appealing. I was looking at them when she spoke.

"We should get together anyway, catch up," she said. "Me and Melanie, you and whoever. Are you seeing anyone?"

"Nobody special," I said. "And it would be great to catch up." I gave Nicola my widest smile.

In response, she took off her hat and ruffled her fair hair, which was shoulder-length but currently tied in a ponytail.

"Cool. I'll see if I can work something out in between organising the wedding and working. If Melanie can't make it, it'll just have to be you and me, like old times."

Which old times was she referring to? The one in the library, where we'd shared that kiss that changed my life? Just thinking about it made me want to do it all again, right there on the pavement before I'd even had my morning coffee. I felt a rush of desire spreading like fire through my body, which was ironic, seeing as Nicola was meant to put fires out, not start them. But she never had where I was concerned.

Oh Nicola Sheen, what do you do to me? Even after all these years.

"I would love that," I replied. *And I would love to kiss you again, feel you pressed against me.*

"And next time—" Nicola said, stroking my arm with her right hand.

I jolted slightly at her touch. "Yes?"

"—Next time, maybe opt for porridge?" And then she gave me a wink.

If I didn't know better, I'd say Nicola Sheen was flirting with me.

"I'll do that," I said before giggling like a teenager. Which in that moment, I was.

Nicola's colleague interrupted us — he was sporting a bushy moustache which was either a hangover from Movember or an ill-advised fashion statement.

"We can take one rig back to the station now and the other can follow — you okay with that, boss?"

"Yep, sounds like a plan."

I opened my eyes wider. Nicola was the boss. A fire *chief*. How incredibly sexy.

"Good to see you," Nicola said. "But next time, let's do it without a fire in tow?" She raised a delicious eyebrow in my direction.

"We can certainly try," I replied.

Nicola turned to her colleague and they strode back towards their bright red vehicle. I watched her retreating figure all the way, before she turned around and jogged back to me, fishing her phone from her pocket.

"Should we... exchange numbers or something? So we can get in touch?" She waved her phone in the air in front of me.

I nodded, fishing in my bag for mine. "Sure, good idea."

"You know, you're not supposed to grab personal items when there's a fire alarm," she added.

"When you're the firestarter, I think different rules apply."

She held me with her gaze as I took the phone from her hands and began to punch in my number. Only a highly-trained eye would be able to tell my hands were shaking slightly. It only took a few seconds, and when I looked back up, her gaze was still on me, all-encompassing, total.

I wanted to tip-toe across the thread that was drawing us back together, to try and unravel what this all meant.

Did Nicola turning up here mean anything? Or was it just pure coincidence? Whatever, Nicola's intense stare told me she was trying to figure it out too.

Neither one of us spoke.

Then Nicola broke the silence. "It's good to see you again, Victoria."

Victoria. Nobody called me that apart from my mum. And of course, Nicola. She'd once told me she loved the name and to shorten it would be a crime, so Victoria it was. When it came out of my mum's mouth, I hated it. But when it came out of her mouth — it still made me wilt. It had back then, and it did now. She was smiling at me again now, but I couldn't read her expression. Did Nicola have any regrets? I would love to have known.

I pressed the green button so that Nicola had my number, then when the call connected, I handed back her phone.

She gave me a small salute. "See you soon."

Then she sprinted back to her vehicle, cracked the engine and ploughed back into the London morning traffic.

I watched her go and managed not to wave in a pathetic fashion.

I tried not to believe in fate and destiny, but sometimes, it had a way of making you sit up and take notice.

* * *

"Nicola Sheen is a firefighter? You're kidding me!"

Holly was cooking dinner for us — fish tacos, which was one of my favourites from her repertoire. She was hunched over the frying pan as usual, her long, lean frame dealing with life from a high vantage point.

I drummed my fingers on the kitchen counter as I grinned at her. "I was as surprised as you when she jumped off the fire engine, believe me." I paused. "Meanwhile, Maureen was less than pleased with me."

Holly cleared her throat. "I can't say I blame her." She moved the cod around the pan, before adding the seasoning mix. "So I take it you were cool, calm and collected and didn't blush like a school girl?" She didn't look over to see my reaction.

"I was as a matter of fact, cool as a cucumber. She told me off, we had a chat about how I should eat porridge and then she went on her way. End of story." Holly didn't need to know all the facts, she'd just disapprove. She's not so hot on fate or destiny.

Holly turned her head. "Really? You didn't ask her if she still loves you like you love her?"

I wafted a hand nonchalantly through the air. "Nope. I was the picture of maturity. Well, as mature as you can be after you've burnt toast and managed to evacuate your building."

Holly glanced my way as she cooked, and I could see she was wondering whether to believe me, and also how far she should probe.

"Well good, if that's the case," she said, slotting the tacos in the hot oven. "I'm proud of you." She turned and looked me in the eye, a hint of something I couldn't quite place held in her gaze. "Maybe you were listening to me the other day." She paused. "Although, I can't see how you managed to contain yourself. Especially if she was in her fire gear — you're gaga for a woman in uniform at the best of times."

I rummaged in the cutlery drawer to set the table. "Who isn't? Don't tell me you wouldn't be interested if your first love strode out of a fire truck and into your life?"

Holly tilted her head and grinned. "I guess it would have a certain *je ne sais quoi*." She paused. "A hot firefighter turning up at my work would have been very welcome today. A little light relief from the stresses of modern life."

"Who was it who was lecturing me on love the other day? Perhaps you need to start a little fire at your work and see who turns up."

"If it's Nicola Sheen, that would be *way* too complex," she said, laughing. "Besides, I heard a rumour she's engaged."

I swiped at Holly with a tea towel. "Ha ha — you know what I mean. You need to be ready for love when it comes along and that might be tomorrow. Romance and self-help books make me open to it." I pointed to my chest. "When love comes knocking, I'm going to have the flat ship-shape, I'll have flossed and my hair will be perfect. I'm going to be ready."

Holly turned off the pan, lifted the fish on to a plate and squeezed lime juice over the top. "I'll be perfectly ready, thanks." She didn't look up. "And I won't be the one searching through my pile of exes for someone to love." She retrieved the taco shells and carried the tomatoes, lettuce and guacamole to our small dining table, pushed up against the left wall of our lounge.

I grabbed a couple of beers from the fridge and followed her to the table.

"But I'm not going to argue with you now — not after I've cooked this lovely dinner. In the meantime, while you're dusting off and updating your Nicola Sheen fantasies, what's in store for the rest of this week? Any more dates in the pipeline?" Holly bit into her taco and the crunch may well have been heard in Yorkshire.

"I do. Tomorrow I have Jenny, an Australian web designer. And then on Thursday, I have a woman called Spanish_Vixen89. I'm holding out high hopes for her."

Holly nodded, swallowing her food before replying. "She sounds like she might be a sultry Mediterranean lady. Or she sounds like she might be 89."

"I've seen her picture, so I'm assuming she was born in 1989."

"And if she turns out to be 89?"

"Then she's looking really good and it makes a fantastic story to tell. Plus, don't be so ageist — she might be absolutely lovely." I crunched into my tacos and savoured the flavours — fish, lime, coriander, avocado and spices — they were delicious. Holly was going to make someone a perfect wife. "So you see, I'm getting on with life and

I am not at all focused on Nicola Sheen who is marrying Melanie Taylor. In fact, I couldn't be happier for them."

Holly nodded her head slowly. "If you say it enough times, you might actually believe it."

I stuck out my tongue at her.

"So, I have a question." Holly was holding up one finger to demonstrate that fact.

"Shoot," I replied, licking my bottom lip to rescue some stray guacamole.

"What happens if you hit it off with both Jenny *and* Spanish Vixen? How will you choose?"

I chewed my mouthful and wrinkled my nose. "I'll worry about that when it happens. If it does, it would be a miracle."

Holly laughed. "And did you get the Dixie Chicks tickets in all the excitement you had at work?" Her face told me she had absolutely zero faith I'd remembered to do it.

I nodded. "I did — two tickets booked. You shall go to the ball."

Holly gave me a dazzling grin, showing off her seriously perfect teeth. "This is going to be the best Christmas run-up ever — Dixie Chicks playing so close to my birthday. I cannot wait!"

9

Tuesday December 6th

I wasn't messing Holly around — I was still on a quest for a Christmas girlfriend. And to prove it, tonight I was turning my attention to Jenny, who was not from the block, but rather from West London.

Jenny was a web designer in a corporate bank, but apart from that, she fitted the Aussie label to a tee. She had smooth, treacle-toned skin that went on for days, freckles across her nose and shoulder-length fair hair that was conditioned to within an inch of its life — I didn't spot one solitary split end. Her sentences still went up at the end even though she'd lived in London for three years, and she had a habit of shortening words, Aussie style. Afternoon became arvo, ambulance became ambo. It was an endearing quality that made me smile.

We met near Liverpool Street at a pop-up food park — one of those London peculiarities that people from outside the city would scoff at. A disused car park, it was now stuffed with food trucks, drinks stands and punters, with hundreds of multi-coloured Christmas lights strung all around, along with an abundance of metal umbrella heaters to ward off the cold. We stood near a burrito van with our mugs of mulled cider, our breath writing messages in the air around us. The speakers were blaring out a procession of Christmas hits, currently a personal favourite, The Pogues And Kirsty MacColl's 'Fairytale Of New York'. I sung the last chorus out loud, swaying my cider back and forth.

"You've got a good voice," Jenny said.

I smiled modestly. "Thanks." Ten points to Jenny.

"Have you been on many dates through the app?" She shivered as she spoke, which I found cute. I've no idea why she was shivering though as she appeared to be dressed in what I can only describe as a duvet — her coat honestly seemed to be 100-tog all the way around.

"A few," I said. "But this is definitely the most Christmassy one yet. I mean, Santa statues, Christmas tunes and fake snow. You could almost forget you were in a car park in London and believe you were in Lapland, couldn't you?"

Jenny laughed. "Very nearly." She paused, looking around. "I still love this though, you know? The Christmas lights, the cold, the snow — even if it is fake. That's what drew me to your ad — the Christmas theme."

I smiled. "I'm glad. Christmas has always been my favourite time of year, hands down." An image of my dad in a Santa hat popped into my head. I pushed it away.

"I love Christmas in Oz too, with the barbies on the beach in your shorts and thongs," Jenny added. "But Christmas as depicted in all the films and songs is cold, so it's great to experience it. When I go back to Oz, I plan to buy some fake snow."

"Do you have plans to move back soon?"

She nodded. "Not imminent, but I only have a five-year visa. So it's going to be in the next couple of years." She looked me dead in the eye. "Unless I find a gorgeous English wife to persuade me otherwise, of course. I'm open to offers."

Jenny gave me a lazy smile, and then before I could think of an appropriate riposte, she kissed me. Her lips were moist and she tasted of alcoholic apples and cinnamon.

When she pulled away a few seconds later, I opened my eyes, surprise radiating from them. I'd only had one drink but the car park spun with possibility. I grinned. "That's what I like about Aussies — never shy about coming forward."

She licked her lips, then dropped her gaze to my lips once more before replying. "I always figure if you find someone you like, you shouldn't leave it ambiguous, or wait till you're both too drunk to remember. You should let them know straight off the bat — no messing. And I like you, you're cute. Plus, you're very English, and I *love* English."

My smile grew wider. "Is that right?" I replied. "Well I couldn't be more English if I tried, so you're in luck!" I skipped over my dad's Spanish roots for the purpose of story-telling for tonight. My mum was from Croydon, so I was sure that tipped the balance.

I poured the contents of my mug down my throat and held it up. "You want some more?" I asked.

Jenny smirked at me before pressing her lips to mine once more. I could get used to this.

After a few seconds she pulled back, her breath still on my face, her eyelids fluttering wildly.

"Yes, please," she replied.

I'd never heard a woman purr before, but there was a first time for everything.

***

After drinks and an incredible burrito from the food truck of the moment, we'd decamped to the outdoor pop-up disco next door, bumping and grinding in our coats and hats, breath circling above us, mulled cider cooling in our mugs. The air was rich with the smell of hot, sugary drinks and pine ferns, and we were on a magical Christmas journey that ended with a Tube back to Jenny's place.

We re-emerged to street level just after 10.30pm, the night air holding an extra chill now. Jenny's house was only five minutes' walk away, but it wasn't until we got inside that I realised how much she was living the Aussie London dream, sharing the house with nine other people.

Our magical Christmas date bubble burst with a loud bang when we walked into the lounge and found a slew of bodies on the sofas and floor watching *The Big Bang Theory*. The room smelt of cheap deodorant and beer.

"Hey everyone — this is Tori." Jenny twirled me around as if she'd just bought me in a shop.

There was a general murmur of hello from the group.

"Okay, see ya later!"

Jenny took my hand once more and led me into the kitchen, which reminded me of student days gone by. The counters were stacked with dirty dishes, the sink full too, and overhead, an old-fashioned washing line was full of someone's off-white underwear. I wasn't sure the kitchen was the best place to be drying laundry.

Jenny, however, took it all in her stride. "Hazards of living with so many people!"

She smiled, handed me a glass of water and led me up two flights of stairs to her room, which was compact to say the least. Squeezed into the space was her unmade double bed shoved against a wall, an Ikea wardrobe and a small desk which was overflowing with empty water bottles and jewellery — rings, necklaces and bracelets. Plus, lying on the small slice of floor running down the right of her double bed was a pink sleeping bag, scrunched up and lying on top of a yoga mat.

I pointed towards it. "You expecting company?"

She nodded. "Yeah — my friend Edie is staying at the moment. She's over from Sydney for a month, but we've got too many people in the lounge so she's taking my floor." Jenny paused, then kissed me again. Her lips were dry. "Don't worry though," she added. "Edie knows the score, so she won't disturb us. If I bring someone back, she knows to give me some space."

Thump — another blow to my ego. I was just another in a long line of Jenny hook-ups. Even Edie was in on the secret, and she'd been here less than a month. I'd fallen for Jenny's lines and now here I was, about to have sex with her. Or I could leave. *Should I leave?* Then again, Jenny was attractive and I'd always been taught never to look a gift horse in the mouth. I wasn't about to start now.

It turned out that Jenny was a one-woman sexual whirlwind — she hadn't waited to kiss me, and she didn't stand on ceremony in the bedroom either. Within minutes, my shirt was off and she was sucking my breasts between her teeth, her hands roaming my back. This was a well-rehearsed routine. Another five minutes and I was naked, lying flat on my back on her bed, Jenny looming above me. Her hair fell on to my breasts and all this without shedding a single stitch of clothing. Jenny was *such* a top.

And then she tried to fuck me, only she kept hitting the target, then missing.

Honestly, she *kept* missing. It took me back to my early years, almost making me feel nostalgic. *Almost.*

"Ow!" I said, jumping as her fingers stabbed me for the third time. We'd drunk a few ciders so I wasn't expecting finesse, but this was something else.

"Sorry!" she mumbled.

After the fourth time of asking, I reached down.

"Try this," I said, guiding her fingers in.

She grinned lazily at me.

However, once she got her bearings, there was no let up from the steam train that was Jenny. She was on a mission to make me come and I was down with that. After her initial fumbling, Jenny remembered what to do and had me sliding to a climax precisely 14 minutes after I'd first entered her bedroom. I know, because Jenny's bedside alarm clock told me so.

Before I could get my breath back, Jenny was naked and on top of me, grinding into me. She leaned forward, her breasts falling on to mine, covering my neck with kisses. And then she began to nip at my neck. And then suck on it, hard, with her teeth.

I flinched. Was she trying to give me a hickey? Had I time-travelled back to my teens?

I pushed her off and she looked surprised, her mouth hanging open, her eyes still hungry.

"You not into that?" she asked in a slurred drawl.

I shook my head. "Not so much."

She threw back her head and chuckled. "Okay, we can just cut straight to the chase," she replied, lowering her mouth back to my neck and then my ear, this time giving me feather-light kisses. "And if you hurry, you can still get the last Tube home."

How's that for a bucket of cold water on my libido?

Still, Jenny's perky breasts and flat stomach went some way to reigniting my desire. I cupped her arse, then slid up and into her — she was so ready. I slid my tongue into her welcoming mouth and began a rhythm with my fingers — I was feeling something of a stud as Jenny moaned above me, her wetness sliding down my hand.

Then she sat up, threw her head back, and began to chant while riding me. When I say chant, it was more like shouting. She was *really* bellowing out the words for everyone to hear. I was thankful we were on the second floor. If she had the room next to the lounge, I'm sure half of them would have been joining us by now. As it was, they were all probably used to this sideshow.

"Oh! Yes!" Jenny shouted, levering herself up and down.

There was only me and her in the room, but it felt like we had an audience.

"Deeper! I love it! Fuck! Me! Harder!" And then she became erratic, bouncing up and down on me now with a staccato rhythm. With every movement of her body, another word spurted out of her mouth.

"I! Love! Having! Sex! With! Women!"

Oh. My. God. She really had just said that. Who the hell was this woman? I narrowed my eyes. *Focus.*

My concentration clearly paid dividends, because within minutes Jenny's muscles were spasming and her insides clutching my fingers, then Jenny was arching her back and crying out. Up high, with her breasts bouncing, she was just the sort of woman I went for. Eventually, she grew tired and lay down beside me, her head lolling lazily in my direction, a half-smile on her face.

"You're okay, you know that?" she said.

I couldn't think of anything to say.

Just then, there was a knock at Jenny's door.

"Who is it?" she said.

"Edie!" a voice replied.

"Open!" Jenny shouted back.

What? With us lying naked and uncovered, in a cloud of sex? Was she fucking crazy?

I sat up, scrabbling to grab the duvet from the bottom of the bed, when in walked Jenny's room-mate, Edie. She looked like she'd just rocked up off an Aussie beach, all blonde tangled hair and brown limbs.

She smiled at us as if this was an everyday occurrence — it crossed my mind it might be.

"Just getting that black top, Jen, sorry!" Her voice was sing-song and didn't carry an ounce of apology. She rummaged in Jenny's wardrobe, before finding the top and holding it up. "Ta-da!" she said, before backing out of the room. "Please," she said, shutting the door with a grin. "Get back to whatever it was you were doing."

Jenny took her at her word, and before I had a chance to speak, she was straddling me again, pushing my hand back inside her. The woman was insatiable. And slightly unhinged. Jenny began to grind herself up and down on top of me.

How long did I have before she started screaming again?

I glanced at the clock: 10.58.

Jenny was right.

If we hurried, I would be able to catch the Tube home.

10

Wednesday December 7th

Holly was leaning against the kitchen counter and grinning at my story. "So are you seeing her again?"

I rolled my eyes. "Absolutely. I mean, who could resist the lesbian bucking bronco? She nearly broke my bloody hand." I massaged my knuckles and flexed my hand as I said it, but even I had to laugh at the comedy of it all.

"It's a great story to tell, you have to admit," Holly replied, smiling.

"Hmmm," I replied. "Maybe in a month or so. But for now, it's still a little too raw." I paused. "Mind you, it was definitely a first — whispering the Tube times in my ear just after I came. She was original, I'll give her that."

Holly let out a bark of laughter this time. "Perhaps you were the early shift."

"Reassuring, thanks."

"Go back, just for me," she said, pumping her fists up and down in excitement. "Just to see what she's got in store for date two. You don't know — maybe she'll invite her flatmate to join in." Holly shot me a wink.

I laughed, then shook my head. "It crossed my mind that's what was going to happen at the time — that this was a set-up. And what could I have done at that point? I was naked and weak — I'd just *come*."

Holly shrugged. "You could have thanked the lesbian goddesses and embraced the moment," she said. "You really have picked them so far, though. Perhaps you need some help with your vetting process."

I ran my tongue along my top lip. "Perhaps you're right."

Holly ripped the top off a breakfast yoghurt and licked it clean. "Anyway, I have some news." She was suddenly bashful. "Spurred on by your actions, I have a date tonight too — she's five years younger than me and she likes badminton. So if all else fails, I've got a new badminton partner."

"That's the spirit," I replied. "Reach for the stars and you might land in Milton Keynes."

Holly waved her yoghurt spoon at me. "Shuddup."

"What's this woman's name?"

Holly blushed. "You don't want to know."

"I do," I said, interest piqued. "What is it?"

Holly shook her head. "It's bizarre."

I furrowed my brow and shook my head. "What's she called?"

Holly took a deep breath. "Her name's Ivy."

I burst out laughing. "You're joking. Holly and Ivy?"

Holly started to laugh now, nodding. "It's ridiculous, I know."

"Or fated. You'd make the front page of the papers if you got married. Especially if you did it on Christmas Day." I clapped my hands with glee.

Holly finished up her yoghurt and chucked the carton in the bin. "Yes, thank you, but she's probably going to hate me on sight. Or she's doing it for a laugh." She paused. "But anyway, back to you — when are you going out with Spanish Vixen lady?"

I sipped my coffee. "Tomorrow — I have a night off tonight. And if you're going to be out with *Ivy*, I can do what I like, can't I? I might lounge around here naked, sipping champagne and eating sushi." As soon as I said it, I had a vision of Nicola Sheen lounging on the sofa beside me, dressed in her full uniform, begging me to strip it off. My cheeks coloured and I crossed my legs as my clit twitched into life.

Holly fixed me with an intense stare. "Nakedness *and* champagne? Maybe I should call off my date and stay in," she said.

"You can't stand Ivy up. Ivy of all people," I said, giving her a wink.

Holly shook her head, bent down and kissed me on the cheek. Her head stayed near mine for a couple of seconds longer than I expected, and the look she gave me sent a shiver down my spine.

The kind of shiver normally reserved for Nicola Sheen.

The kind of shiver I didn't normally associate with Holly.

A question mark hung in my mind and I saw the same one reflected back in Holly's face. It was all too much to process before I'd even had a coffee.

"Have a good day," I said, my voice sketchy.

She held my gaze. "You too."

Her shoes squeaked as she twisted on the kitchen floor, as though about to say something, but then checked herself. Instead, Holly disappeared out the door.

I had no idea what had just happened, but I was slightly breathless.

***

I didn't opt for the nakedness in the end — it always sounds more glamorous than the reality. Instead, I watched a soppy Christmas film, heated a pizza and drank the end of a lovely red we had leftover from the weekend, followed by two mince pies with cream. I toasted my dad as I ate them, and hoped that wherever he was, they celebrated Christmas too.

It was good to have some space, good to have some time to myself. And whenever my mind wandered, it always seemed to stray back to the same topic: Nicola Sheen. Who certainly wasn't the teenage dreamboat I recalled, but she still had something. She had charisma, she had my memories, she had me. And she had Melanie Taylor.

I picked up my phone and scrolled through to Nicola's number, staring at it, willing her to ring. But why would she? She was engaged, after all. Yet there had definitely been something the other day — something in her eyes. Something that told me she was curious, just like I'd been. Where might things have gone if circumstances had been different? If we'd kissed in my bedroom all those years ago, for instance, and not in the library? She might not have run so quickly, that's for sure.

I threw my phone down on the sofa and went to make a cup of tea, grabbing a couple of biscuits from the barrel on my way back. It was lovely to just sit and relax and not have to be on a first date. First dates were draining — especially when they involved sex.

When I sat back down, I had a text — was it Holly making sure I was decent? No, it was from Nicola Sheen.

'Hi, I'm in your area tomorrow pm. Fancy a coffee & a catch-up? Nicola.'

A coffee and a catch-up. What did that mean? Was coffee code for something else? Was it wrong to hope that it was? I scanned my social calendar, but remembered I had a date with Spanish_Vixen89 tomorrow night. Damn. Should I cancel? No, I probably shouldn't.

Besides, Nicola Sheen was engaged.

I texted back to tell her I had plans tomorrow night, but she told me this was an afternoon coffee date, so I agreed.

Tomorrow, I was having coffee with the woman who altered the course of my life, followed by drinks with a Spanish Vixen.

Tomorrow seemed monumental already.

11

Thursday December 8th

Nicola turned up puffed and dishevelled from bridal shopping and in need of a pick-me-up. We'd arranged to meet at a coffee shop round the corner from my work and Nicola's face spelled tiredness: her eyes were shaded grey, her skin dry, her nose runny. She needed an energy boost, along with a plate of superfoods and some quality concealer. However, as I really didn't know her that well, I decided to keep that to myself.

We sat down with our lattes.

"You okay?" I asked, even though it was plain she wasn't.

She gave me a pained smile. "It's just been a weird day, and it's not something I can really speak to Melanie about. Wedding dress shopping is freaking me out. Reminding me of the first time round." She took a sip of her coffee and recoiled — it was too hot.

I stared at her. "First time round?" What the hell was she talking about?

She pursed her lips and nodded. "I keep forgetting we haven't seen each other in a while."

I shook my head. "Quite a long while."

"I suppose it is." She paused. "I was married before. To a man. I was young, I got pregnant, he proposed, it seemed the right thing to do." She shrugged. "One of those things, but it's freaked me out a bit today."

I managed to stop my mouth from dropping open — this was a lot to take in. "You've been married before and you have a child?"

She nodded again, looking wary.

"I can see why wedding shopping might be odd for you then." I sipped my latte, trying to make sense of my jumbled emotions. "So when did you… switch sides? Is Melanie your first?" I was going to break down and sob on the table if she said yes.

Nicola shook her head. "No, she's not." She paused. "When we were friends, there was something there, didn't you think? That was my first inkling, anyway."

She was even a little bit hesitant when she said it — she wasn't sure if I remembered. She had absolutely *no idea* just how much I remembered.

I remembered all of it. Every single little detail.

"I mean, have you ever thought about us since then? I have. When we kissed in the library… I was just, too scared. Too scared to contemplate it. So I went for the easier option."

If I'd been worried we'd be stuck for small talk, it

turned out I needn't have been concerned. Nicola Sheen didn't do small talk. My head was spinning just trying to keep up.

"The easier option was getting pregnant?" I raised an eyebrow as I said it.

She grimaced. "No, that bit I didn't plan. But it seems like I get pregnant at the drop of a hat, so that's one of the upsides of switching teams. I don't need to worry about that anymore." She didn't look me in the eye.

"As soon as we kissed, I knew I was gay," I said. "No boy had ever made me feel like that." Apparently I didn't do small talk today either. I stared at the table, not daring to look up. Her gaze was already scorching the side of my face. "So yes, I've thought about you since, which is why I was so surprised when you turned up the other night. And that you were marrying Melanie."

She gazed at me and bit her lip. "I know. Which is why I thought we should meet up. Because of how we left things."

"Badly?" *So badly, I wanted to curl up on the library floor and never move again?* Did she know my whole world shifted, and then she just whipped the rug from underneath me and walked away without a single look back?

I picked up the small pink packet of sugar lounging in my saucer, folded the top, then put it down again. All the while, I avoided Nicola's gaze. If she wanted me to just consign our kiss to history and not acknowledge what it was, I couldn't. Our kiss made me realise I was a lesbian.

Our kiss meant something. Still, it upset me how much it still meant. Maybe Holly had a point — maybe I did cling on to things.

When I eventually risked looking at Nicola, her face was hesitant. "I had no choice but to leave — my parents were adamant." She sighed and fidgeted with her spoon. "And then after I left and had the miscarriage, I went to sixth form and met Callum. He was lovely. But I got pregnant again within a year, he proposed and I said yes." She shrugged. "But it was never going to work, because, well…"

"You're gay?" I finally glanced in her direction to see her answer.

She nodded. "Yes, because I'm gay. Callum was pretty good about it all really, considering. We still see each other because of Heath, but that's it."

"And you met Melanie online?"

She nodded. "I had a couple of girlfriends before her — being a firefighter is a help, women throw themselves at you."

I cleared my throat. "I bet."

"But Melanie, she was just… different. And I'm ready to put down some roots. And I want the stability for Heath too — a loving home with two parents."

If Nicola was thinking she'd have a stable home with Melanie involved, I didn't want to be the one to break it to her that she might not be the perfect person to pick.

"How old's Heath?" I said, changing the subject.

"Six — I'll show you a picture." She fished her iPhone out of her bag and pulled up a photo of a gap-toothed boy with both thumbs up.

"He looks like you." And he did — the same almond eyes, the same mouth.

She smiled. "Everyone says that." She drank some more coffee.

I cleared my throat and she looked up.

"What?"

I shook my head. "Nothing."

Nicola crossed her legs and regarded me. "You were going to say something, so please, say it."

I rolled my thoughts around my head. Was honesty always the best policy? Not in my experience.

"It's just… don't you think you're rushing into it a bit with Melanie? You haven't known each other that long, and there's Heath to consider."

Nicola smiled. "And now you're sounding like my mum whose response was exactly that." She looked me in the eye. "But Melanie asked, and sometimes, if something feels right, you just have to take the leap and take a chance. I'm a big believer in that. I took a chance on Callum, but it didn't work. I'm going to give me and Melanie my best shot."

It didn't sound like the ideal premise for a marriage.

"Have you set a date yet?" I was keeping my voice calm despite the fact my insides were jangling.

"New Year's Eve," she said, before holding up her

hands. "And I know what you're going to say — it's too quick. But when you find the right person, why wait?"

The bullet entered my heart with a direct hit. I felt winded, like I was suddenly stranded on a peninsular, with the wind whipping up and the rain closing in. New Year's Eve? That was less than a month away.

"That is quick. Are you sure you're not pregnant again?"

She gave me a look, and now it really was just like old times.

"Can you even get a place to get married at such short notice?"

She waved a hand. "It's not going to be a big do. We're doing registry office and then back to Melanie's parents' house for the reception." She shrugged. "We've both done the big do before, so this will be smaller."

I tried to hold Nicola's gaze.

However, she dropped hers to the table, before taking a deep breath. "Melanie, though — she's great, right?"

She wanted validation of Melanie from me. I searched my brain for something to say.

"She's definitely a one-off," I said.

Nicola smiled. "A one-off. I like that." She paused and placed her hand on my arm. "And you're invited to the wedding, of course."

I jumped at the contact — where Nicola Sheen was concerned, I was still 16.

She squeezed. "And of course, you're welcome to bring a plus one. Did you say you were seeing someone?"

She turned to me and her gaze fell from my eyes, to my lips, then back up again.

My stomach dropped. I shook my head reluctantly. "Not really. I'm dating, but nobody special." I didn't take my eyes off her the whole time, and she didn't budge either.

A warning bell rang in my head, and I was pretty sure I wasn't misreading the signals.

Nicola Sheen might be marrying Melanie Taylor, but right there, she wanted to kiss me.

She licked her lips again, and my breath caught in my throat.

I checked my watch. I still had another two hours till I had to meet my date.

"Do you fancy another coffee?"

She flicked her almond eyes back up. "Love one," she replied, a smile playing on her lips.

***

My date with Spanish Vixen that evening wasn't going to be easy. I'd only left Nicola Sheen an hour ago and my emotions were exhausted after the extended workout she'd given them — first loves will do that to you. Plus, Jenny was still a fresh, slightly queasy memory.

I don't know how players do it. I'd only slept with one woman this week and gone for drinks with another, and already I was a multi-tasking failure. As every lesbian knows, keeping one woman happy is hard enough, let alone two or three.

Nicola and I had finished three cups of coffee before she left to meet Melanie for dinner in town, hence I now had a caffeine headache hanging on my brain. The topics had got progressively lighter with each coffee, but I was still stunned she was planning to get married this month, even if her body language was telling me she wasn't ready. This was a new side to Nicola, and one I wasn't particularly in love with.

Logically, I supposed there would be a lot of sides to Nicola that wouldn't exactly thrill me in the present day, but I was still stuck on Nicola Sheen, circa High School. She was a hard habit to break.

I had two friends who'd got married in the past year because they thought it was 'time' and they wanted their life to run to the schedule they'd set in their heads. "I have to be married by the time I'm 28, and my first baby is due at 31," one had told me. When I'd asked them about true love and finding their soulmate, they'd looked at me like I was speaking a language they'd never heard of. "That's all very lovely, Tori," the other had said, shaking her head. "But I live in the *real* world, on *real* time schedules. If you want your life to run to order, you have to look at what you've got, decide if you can live with it and then act or make a change."

Sometimes, my friends depressed me more than I could put into words.

Spanish Vixen and I were meeting in Covent Garden at one of those bars that promise to do American diner food really well, but normally leave you with nothing more than a sad taste in your mouth. Still, they had a happy hour, so all was not lost. My heels clip-clopped across the cobbles as I made my way across Covent Garden's main square. The market stalls were just packing up as I passed them, and the scent of anticipation and roasted chestnuts coated the air. To my right, a unicyclist was juggling knives and telling the crowd a story of the last time he did this and how he nearly died.

I scanned the bar as I went in, but couldn't see any sign of my date — at least, nobody who matched her profile picture of dark Latin looks, long shiny hair and a smile that radiated confidence.

Nicola Sheen had left me reeling with her revelations: she was a divorcee and a mum already, and on top of that, she remembered our kiss. Plus, from her body language, she wanted to relive it just as much as I did. However, I was starting to have doubts about my feelings towards Nicola. What else didn't I know about her? If I thought about myself aged 16 to now, I guessed the answer would be quite a lot.

I didn't have much time to dwell on my thoughts, though, as my date arrived bang on time. She was shorter than me, only by a couple of inches, but she was way more glossy, with yards of white teeth shining out from olive skin. She took my hand and shook it firmly, but her eyes avoided direct contact. Perhaps she was shy.

"Nice to meet you Vixen — I'm Tori." I still wore my

best smile. "Can I get you a drink? I might be Christmassy and have a mulled wine."

She sat on the stool beside me, fighting with it to get comfortable. "I don't do red wine — stains the teeth." She smoothed down her black skirt and crossed her shapely legs. "I'll have a white wine, though."

I ordered her a glass of Sauvignon Blanc and a Malbec for me. I knew drinking wine on an empty stomach was a bad idea, but I'd deal with that later.

Vixen's real name turned out to be Max, which was the name of our dog when I was growing up, so slightly off-putting. When I asked her what she did, she told me sales, but then asked about my work. I filled her in on my marketing job and she smiled in all the right places, but there was something about Max that just wasn't quite right. Was she already in a relationship? One of those women who just liked to come out on dates to remind themselves they still had it? I couldn't put my finger on it.

It wasn't until the second glass of wine that I found out exactly what wasn't quite right with Max, when she produced a green folder and spread some papers out across our table.

"What's this?" I asked.

And then Max came alive. "This," she said, wafting a hand across the papers, "is the key to your future. This is my bullet-proof insurance scheme." She grinned at me and flicked her hand right, then left. "I weighed up bringing this out on the date, but I figured I couldn't let this one slide because I want to share this opportunity with everyone I meet. And I've got a good feeling about you — about *us*."

I was confused. "Sorry, you've lost me."

Max shook her head. "Do you currently have insurance for yourself and your job?"

"What?"

"What happens if you lose your job? The economy's very uncertain, do you have savings put aside to pay your rent or your mortgage?"

I held up a palm to stop her in her tracks. It didn't work. Max was on a roll and nobody was going to stop her. Our date was just a stage and I was the audience.

"What about if you get a terminal illness and need 24-hour care — you can't rely on the NHS anymore," she continued.

"Max!" I almost shouted. Okay, maybe I shouted a little. The man at the next table turned to me and frowned. I ignored him. "Are you honestly trying to sell me insurance on a blind date? Is this what you use this app for?"

She leaned over and put a hand on my arm. "I'm not trying to sell to you. I'm trying to save you so much heartache in your future. Think of me as your fairy godmother looking out for *you*. I'm on your side, which you'll see when you look at our stunning terms and conditions," she said, lifting up one of the forms.

I stood up, shaking my head and gathering my coat.

I was close to laughing out loud at the situation. I mean, I'd heard about the perils of online dating, but honestly? So far, I was a walking encyclopedia of how not to do it. Perhaps I *should* let Holly choose my dates from now on.

Max frowned up at me. "You're going?" she said. "But I don't think you understand — you can't afford to walk away from me. This deal is too good to be true!"

Now I did allow myself a little laugh. "It's a risk I'm willing to take," I told her, putting a hand on my hip. "Tell me, are you even a lesbian or is this just a way of approaching new clients?" I shrugged my coat on, staring at Max.

Her face stayed calm, not reacting to my imminent departure at all. She looked me in the eye, stood up and gave me the fakest of fake smiles. "I'm 100 per cent lesbian, sweetheart. And if you buy a policy from me and stick around, I'll prove it to you and give you the best orgasm of your life, guaranteed. What do you say?" She winked at me before holding up the form again, this time along with a pen.

I wondered how many times Max had used that line, and more to the point, how many times it'd worked. I'd *love* to have known.

She was slick, I had to hand it to her. It was almost a shame I wasn't going to experience *all* that Max had to offer.

Almost, but not quite.

***

I was so glad to be home after the day I'd had — emotional trauma and hilarity of the highest order. I made myself a cup of tea and flicked through the dating app, but I didn't have the energy or the heart to arrange another date. Maybe celibacy was an appealing option after all.

I'd had a text from Jenny today, asking if I fancied meeting up again.

I hadn't replied.

The conversation with Holly yesterday kept playing in my mind and I smiled. Holly always managed to cheer me up, whatever happened.

Just at that moment my phone lit up — I looked down and saw I had a text from Nicola.

At 10.30 at night.

She was thinking about me as she was going to bed. Was she in bed already? Was she naked? Was she thinking about me naked? I felt a rush between my legs as I picked up my phone and swiped.

'Hey — trying the bridal shopping thing again tomorrow. Fancy another coffee after? Really enjoyed catching up today. x'

She'd sent me a kiss — this was a new development.

'Sure, I'd love to. Tomorrow after work?'

But even as I clicked send, I had a tight feeling knotting in my stomach, telling me this was the wrong thing to do. In the distance a red flag was being waved, but I couldn't stop myself. I wanted to see Nicola again. I wanted to hear more words drop from her lips, telling me how much she'd thought about me over the years. I wanted her to say she'd loved me too, just like I'd loved her back then.

Once she said that, I could have closure and move on.

12

Friday December 9th

The next day, I woke up in a happy mood, despite last night's disastrous date. I chalked it up to experience and set about grabbing Friday by the scruff of its neck and kissing it into submission. I even managed to get a seat on the Tube, which proves if you think positively, positive things happen for you. At least, that's what my self-help books told me.

The morning rattled by with a succession of back-to-back meetings with colleagues and clients. I ate lunch in the staffroom and checked my phone, but I hadn't had a text from Nicola about where and when we were meeting that afternoon. I decided to leave the details up to her, play it cool, not be the chaser. I wasn't going to get caught up in this, I'd promised Holly and I was serious. But another quick coffee to discuss her bridal outfit choices wouldn't hurt. Was Nicola going for a full-on white bridal gown or was she going to opt for a stylish suit? Or none of the above?

Sal and I had a final meeting of the day with a new client in Soho. The company were a new start-up business dealing in uber-stylish (read, expensive) kids clothing, and they wanted to boost their internet presence and search engine optimisation (SEO) ranking. In short, they were just the sort of job I loved, because they were always so amazed when what we did worked for them.

People who've never had any experience of the digital space often think that marketing and SEO is made-up mumbo-jumbo — right up until the moment when their sales shoot up and they're left with their jaws hanging open. Sal and I knew exactly what we were doing, we presented well and the clients seemed happy. Now all we had to do was get back to the office, deliver the goods and wait for them to send us the thank you email. It normally happened within a week of the campaign going live.

Sal had to dash straight off from the meeting to pick up her kids, leaving me to walk back to the office through the afternoon hubbub of a festive Friday in Soho. The pavements were already scratched from the previous night and the air was so thick with cold it almost rattled, but my grey woollen scarf was protecting me — it had been a birthday present from Holly last year. Of all the people in my life, Holly was the one who always got my presents right.

I stared in the posh French bakery and marvelled at their cakes and tarts, but I was brought to standstill in the next shop window. A bridal shop, filled with flowing white lacy gowns. And there, standing in the middle of the display was Nicola Sheen, with, I assumed, the shop owner or assistant. Nicola was dressed casually in jeans and a black leather jacket. Her fair hair shone, her face perfectly made-up, and she was wearing biker boots and a thick brown watch. In short, she looked like a dyke dream. Before I knew what I was doing, I knocked on the window.

She turned when she heard and a grin spread across her face as she beckoned me in with her hand, the shop assistant smiling beside her.

I went to go in, then stopped. Was this a good idea, helping to choose the bridal gown of my first love? My brain didn't take long to answer.

No, it wasn't. I ran it through a few of my brain filters, and categorically, they all agreed this was a bad idea. But I went in anyway — how could I not when Nicola Sheen was dressed in leather? I knew the rules to this game, but sometimes, rules were made to be broken.

"Perfect timing!" As I walked through the door, Nicola walked round the woman and enveloped me in a bear hug like we were long-lost friends reuniting for the first time. I caught a waft of her perfume — Calvin Klein? — as well as cigarettes. Did Nicola smoke? I had no idea. In fact, there was so much I didn't know about her.

"Perfect timing for?" She let me go, but her hand was still hanging loose around my waist.

"Telling me what you think about the dress. You remember I was having trouble?"

I nodded.

She swept her hair out of her face and I caught a glimpse of the 16-year-old I'd been in love with all those years ago. Still the same expression of daring, still the same vulnerability that had drawn me into her all that time ago, and was threatening to do so again.

"So what do you think?"

I shook my head. "About what?"

"Coming and telling me whether or not I look like a meringue in these dresses? I mean, Sophie is brilliant, but I could use someone who knows me."

I was just about to take issue with how much I really knew her, but Nicola wasn't waiting for an answer — she was already off down the shop with Sophie in hot pursuit. I followed cautiously, until we got to the dressing room end, a semi-circle with three over-sized changing rooms and comfy pink sofas for guests to sit on. I sat down on one and Nicola went into the middle changing room, before poking her head out of the curtain.

"This first one, I'm not so sure about, so be honest, I don't mind."

I nodded. "Honesty, got it." Even though I was pretty sure that was exactly what no bride *ever* wanted.

The tinkle of the shop door took Sophie away, and then it was just me and Nicola in a sea of white and lace. My life couldn't get much more surreal if it tried.

While I was waiting in this artificial web of happiness, my phone vibrated in my bag. It was a text from Holly asking if I fancied a Friday night beer. I would definitely be in need of a beer after this escapade, so I texted her straight back to say yes.

When I looked up, Nicola was standing in front of me in an off-the-shoulder fishtail gown, looking every inch the bride. She looked at me for a reaction, but I couldn't speak. Seeing that much of her skin was having a strange effect on my vocal chords, causing them to knot together and my breath to quicken. I tried again, but no sound came out.

"You don't like it?" She wrinkled her brow, then walked over to the mirror and regarded herself left, then right. "It's a bit too... Essex d'you think? A bit too bling?"

I shook my head. "No, you look gorgeous. Really. But maybe something more classic would be better?" I hoped this was a safe thing to say. How Nicola looked was beside the point. She was standing in a wedding dress with only me as the audience and this was messing with my head more than I cared to consider. Seeing her in front of me dressed to marry someone else pierced my soul. She'd already cut me open once, and now she was doing it again.

Nicola was oblivious. "You're right, but I thought I'd try this one — I don't hate it as much as I thought I would."

My mind was playing images of Nicola walking down the aisle in the dress, but instead of Melanie waiting at the end, it was me. I shook my head and blinked.

"Let me show you the next one — this is my favourite." Nicola disappeared behind the curtain again and I exhaled loudly.

Sweat was dripping down my back and I'm sure my chest was glowing red under my coat, being battered as it was by my pounding heart.

I could do this. *Breathe*.

Within a minute, Nicola's head popped out again and she looked around before settling on me. "Where's Sophie?"

"She had another customer," I said.

"Right." Nicola gave me a pained smile. "Would you mind giving me a hand with the zip on this one? Sophie did it last time."

I returned her smile right back. "Sure, no problem," I said.

Fuckety fuck.

I left my bag where it was — I figured it was safe in this environment, bridal shops not being known for their smash and grab raids.

But when I got that close to Nicola Sheen's bare back, I was back in High School, back on my bed. Her honeyed skin was smooth and so inviting. I wanted to bend down and kiss it, trail my tongue up that back, then spin her around and… I closed my eyes to stop my mind creating any more thoughts and it half worked. When I reopened them, Nicola had her head turned and was staring at me.

"You okay?" she asked.

I went to speak but no sound came out again. My mouth was gluey, all sense of time and place woozy.

I nodded.

Her eyes dropped to my lips, then back up to my eyes, then she turned quickly.

A blush crept into my cheeks, then slid down my neck and on to my chest. I cleared my throat and kicked into action, removing my gloves and stuffing them in my coat pockets. Then I stood with my hands poised, and eventually, pulled the two sides of the dress together with my left hand and began tugging the zip up with my right. Of course, the action meant I was now in direct contact with Nicola Sheen, my bare fingers on her naked back, but I was pushing that thought to the back of my mind.

I was helping her into her wedding dress. I was a friend helping out and I was going to do my job right.

It only took a few more seconds, and the dress fitted her perfectly — the waist, the arms, the length, everything. It was an off-the-shoulder number, satin and lace, with an elegant, short train. It was understated but undoubtedly classy, exactly what Nicola wanted. Her strong, elegant shoulders stood firm, and when she posed in front of the changing room mirror, she couldn't help but break into a grin. She looked absolutely beautiful, and I told her so, standing to her right.

I stared at both our reflections in the mirror and caught her eye. "It's like it was made for you."

She fluttered her eyelids before fixing me with a

reflected gaze. "I know." Her eyes teared up and her face clouded with sadness.

I panicked. "Hey," I said, putting a hand on the top of either shoulder. "No crying."

She turned slowly, shaking her head and leaned her head on my shoulder, my arm going round her in a painfully awkward embrace. Could she hear my heart thumping in my chest? I hoped not.

"I'm sorry — it just reminds me of before, all the time I've wasted. All the time I could have been living the life I should have been leading, instead of being miserable with boyfriends and pretending to be something I'm not."

I patted her back awkwardly — I got what she was saying, but it still didn't make the situation any less odd. All I wanted to do was agree with her, tell her that yes, you did make the wrong decision, you did walk away from me and the best thing that could have happened to you. And now you're standing in a wedding dress marrying someone else? Pick me!

But I didn't say any of that, although the way my chest was churning, she might have picked up on the body language. Instead, I gently held her at arm's length and looked her in the eye.

"We've all got what-ifs, you know," I said. "I've been out with some really unsuitable women, and my last girlfriend, I broke her heart. So if you think being gay stops you from making bad decisions, you're wrong."

She smiled at that.

A tear rolled down her cheek and I wiped it away with my finger.

She followed my finger as I removed it, then fixed me with her almond eyes again. *Those eyes*.

"I walked away from you," she whispered. "What would have happened if I hadn't walked away from you?"

My mind was like one of those kaleidoscope toys I used to play with as a child, whirling round and round. I didn't want to answer because I didn't know what the answer was. I knew what the make-believe answer was, but…

It happened before I could stop it. At least that's what I told myself afterwards.

No sooner had those words tumbled from her mouth than she was moving towards me, her mouth now centimetres from mine. She checked my eyes, then my mouth, then pressed her lips to mine.

Her lips were exactly as I remembered them — without a word, they whispered sweet nothings to me. Her kiss was slow, soft and sensual as she caressed my lips with a surety of touch. Nicola's lips were silky smooth and she was pitch perfect. I was locked into Nicola's world, and she to mine. I was helpless.

My eyes were closed, my body in a state of frenzy, even though I was standing perfectly still. But Nicola Sheen was kissing me like her life depended on it, so I wasn't about to stop her in her tracks. This had been my fantasy for years.

Apart from the bit where she's standing in a wedding dress, about to marry someone else, but life's never perfect, is it?

I was sinking, but her kiss was keeping me afloat. She tasted of sparkle and promise.

"How you getting on in there?" a voice asked. It was Sophie.

We both jolted and pulled away from each other, Nicola wiping her mouth before straightening herself up in front of the mirror.

"Really good — I really like this one," she said, not missing a beat. "And I think Victoria likes it too, don't you?"

I nodded. "Really lovely," I said, my voice croaky.

Nicola took another huge breath, then pulled back the curtain and strode out into the shop where Sophie was making positive noises.

"I think this is the one." Nicola was nodding at herself in the huge mirror while I was still standing in the changing room. I was scared to go out there. Wouldn't Sophie know, wouldn't everyone know? Weren't we lit up with guilt for all to see?

"You look gorgeous, that dress is spot-on," said another voice. I walked out with as much poise as I could muster, and smiled at the other customer who was now joining in the dress approval ritual.

Nicola twirled in the big changing room, soaking up the attention, not ever catching my eye.

My mouth was still on fire, I could still feel her tongue inside me.

She was playing the part perfectly, which I found disconcerting to say the least. But then, she always was far more theatrical than me, able to style things out.

But now, having just shared that kiss, I could see her whole life was one big act, with Nicola Sheen lurching from one scene to the next. Who was the real Nicola? I had no idea. All I knew was, I needed some air, to get out of there sharpish. Kissing my first love had thrown up a tornado of emotions.

"Nicola, I've got to go — got to get back to work." I walked over to the pink sofa and picked up my bag, wiping my mouth with the back of my hand as I did. It didn't stop my mouth burning. "That's definitely the one, though." I pointed towards the dress she was wearing. "You look absolutely stunning."

Nicola turned to me, but her face was hard to read. Was she sad I was leaving? I had no idea, because I could see she was torn — torn between playing the part of the excited bride, and the reality of what had just happened in the changing room. But with an audience watching her, there was only one way this was going to go. Her eyes held mine for a fraction of a second, before she regarded herself in the mirror again and cracked one of her most choreographed smiles yet.

"I think you're right — I think we have a winner."

"Great," I said. "I'll see you soon."

Nicola's panicked gaze honed in on me as I walked over and leaned in to kiss her on the cheek.

She closed her eyes and took a sharp intake of breath before stroking my arm. "See you soon," she said.

I trembled to my core, but still managed to smile at Sophie and walk casually out of the shop. Even though every bone in my body wanted to sprint out of there at 100mph.

***

Holly was sat at her usual table with a few of her workmates when I walked in. The bar was jam-packed as I knew it would be on a Friday night after work, but that was perfect as it took my mind off what had just happened.

"Hey!" Holly got up and pulled me into a hug. "One of my all-time favourite people — let me get you a drink!" She disappeared to the bar and reappeared in record time with a piping hot mulled wine for me. "You okay? You look weird." Her face was flushed and she was peering at me up close.

I shook my head and smiled. "I'm fine — just been a long day. But this," I said, holding up the wine, "is just what the doctor ordered."

Holly grinned. "Just call me Doctor Holly!"

Holly shuffled her work colleagues around the table so I could squeeze in. I knew them all pretty well with Holly being the team leader, and they were a friendly bunch. I was glad of their warmth tonight as this was exactly what I needed — to be cocooned and shielded from the mad world outside these walls. In this pub, with these people, I was safe from Nicola Sheen and everything she represented.

"So how was Ivy the other night?" I asked Holly. "You said it was okay on text, but I want the juicy details. Was she creepy? Stained green?"

She smiled at me, but it was in black and white. "She wasn't creepy or green. It's a bit early to tell if we're going to exchange rings and get married any time soon, but you know, it was an okay first date."

"Did you kiss?"

Holly went all coy. "A goodnight kiss — nothing major. But we're going out again tomorrow night, so who knows?" She took a sip of her beer, and looked away briefly. "How about you?"

I shook my head and laughed. "Spanish Vixen was yet another of my disaster dates that I'm thinking about starting a blog about. Perhaps a book too, then a mini-series. I think it'd go down well. A bit like her."

Holly raised an eyebrow. "What happened this time?"

"Let's see," I said, spreading my hands. "She tried to sell me life insurance, and then if I bought it — and only if I bought it — she promised me the best orgasm of my life."

Holly nearly spat her drink out. "That's a unique sell," she laughed.

"It's only a matter of time before she's on *The Apprentice*," I replied, exhaling. After what had just happened in the bridal shop, thinking about Max was light relief.

"You've got her number, right?" Holly was smiling her lopsided smile. "Just in case I have a life insurance emergency."

"On speed dial, of course."

We both smiled at each other.

"And any more dates in the pipeline?"

I shook my head. "I'm a bit dated out, to tell you the truth."

Holly frowned. "But you're on a schedule — you've got to get a girlfriend by Christmas."

I shrugged. "Yeah well, that might have seemed like a good idea initially, but now I'm not so sure. I'm exhausted and not getting anywhere fast, so I might give it a break for a bit. See where life takes me and stop chasing my own tail. I could do with some peace and quiet."

"This is a change of pace," Holly replied. "I thought this was do or die, nobody moves until this project is complete?"

"It was, but now I'm a bit over it. If it happens, it happens. If it doesn't, it's not the end of the world. I'm cool with it."

Holly frowned. "Well I'm not okay with that. You're going to get a girlfriend by Christmas. It's my personal mission."

I took another sip of my mulled wine and gave her a look. "Have you been drinking already?"

She giggled slightly. "Only a couple." Then she put her arm around me and gave me a kiss on the cheek.

The world always felt like a safer, warmer place with Holly's arm around me and I was glad that with the likes of Nicola, Jenny and Max in the world, it was Holly I came home to, Holly who was always there to talk.

I could rely on Holly in ways I could never dream of with anybody else in my life.

13

Saturday December 10th

The following afternoon found me lying on the sofa in the lounge, watching our Christmas tree lights blink on and off, listening to the trains rattle by our window. Sometimes, the noise of the trains drove me insane, but at other times, like today, it was soothing and comforting, providing an order to my day. And I needed order today, because yesterday had been studded with disorder.

I'd kissed Nicola Sheen while she was trying on her wedding dress. Or had she kissed me? However it happened, I didn't come out of it covered in anything resembling glory. But it was a one-off — she was marrying Melanie, so I had to let it go. It was just stupid, pre-wedding jitters. After all, this kind of thing happened with brides and grooms all over the world. It's what stag and hen parties were created for.

I got up and stood at the window, staring into a train below our window, stuck at a signal. Our flat was close enough that you could see people's faces, make out the newspaper they were reading. But you never knew what they were thinking, whether they were looking at you, whether or not they could make out the turmoil embedded into my Saturday. To them, I probably just looked like a normal young woman without a care in the world.

My phone beeped and I grabbed it.

It was a text from Nicola. Okay, so yesterday could be slotted neatly into the pile marked 'pre-wedding nerves'. But today? I didn't know why she was texting me again today. Okay, not 100 per cent true — I had an inkling, but the omens weren't good. I clicked to find out.

'Working today, but wondered if you fancied meeting after work? A quick chat would be good.'

Nicola's texts were always short, sharp and vague. A meet-up. A quick chat. Only things never went quite according to Nicola's plans, did they? I knew I should say no, of course I did. We'd kissed yesterday and she was getting married in three weeks.

My plans today had involved going to the gym, then relaxing after my messy week. Nicola hadn't featured. But then again, I was only going to sit and stew thinking about what had happened, so perhaps meeting up and writing it off would be a good thing? The more I thought about it, the more it made sense. We could talk about it like adults, and put a full stop under it once and for all.

I texted back after I'd made myself a cup of coffee and was sure of my actions. Nicola passed by the flat on her way home, so I gave her my address and told her to stop by after work.

I sat down on the sofa, but couldn't shake the nagging feeling that was sat right beside me.

***

By the time Nicola knocked on the door an hour late at 8pm, I'd managed to work myself up into something of a frenzy. I'd spent the afternoon punching bags and lifting weights in the gym, but it didn't seem to have popped my energy bubble much. At 7.30pm, when Nicola still hadn't shown, I'd decided alcohol was the answer and had poured myself a large gin and tonic. It had taken the edge off my self-infused frazzle, but only the outer corners. The nerve centre was still strapped around my emotions and was ready to explode at any time.

I opened the door to a flustered looking Nicola. "Hi," she said. "I'm so sorry I'm late — paperwork at the station and a bit of a staff issue. I couldn't get away."

My earlier steely resolve melted as she fixed me with her sad eyes and I waved her apology away as if none of it mattered. She was dressed in jeans and a black Fire Dept shirt that accentuated her breasts, and I tried my hardest not to stare for too long. Not quite a full fire uniform, but a hint of one.

"No problem, come in." I stood aside and breathed in Nicola's scent as she walked past me. I could still detect what had drawn me to her all those years ago. Promise.

I led her through the hallway and into the lounge. "Can I get you a drink?"

Nicola took in the lounge. "Wow, I'd forgotten how much you like Christmas. It looks like Santa's grotto in here."

I smiled. "Only comes round once a year."

"Does your dad still go crazy for it too?" she asked.

I dropped my eyes to the floor and inhaled. "He did." I paused. "But he died seven years ago."

Nicola's hand covered her mouth. "Shit — I'm so sorry. I know how close you were." She took a step towards me, but I waved her away.

"You weren't to know — we've been out of each other's lives for a long time." I fixed her with my gaze, letting the words sink in. "Drink?"

Nicola licked her lips. "Beer would be great."

I took one of Holly's from the fridge, knowing she wouldn't thank me for that. Holly was a very generous person, but not when it came to Nicola Sheen.

We sat at opposite ends of the sofa and eyed each other cautiously.

Nicola picked at her beer label before speaking. "So, thanks for agreeing to see me."

"Of course, why wouldn't I?"

The comment hung in the air above us, lit like a neon sign.

We both knew the answer.

Nicola shrugged. "Because the other day wasn't your

typical dress fitting." A train rattled by outside the window and Nicola turned to watch. "Very handy for trains here," she said, still looking out the window. She turned back to me and our eyes met.

I felt a rush between my legs. *Those eyes.*

She shifted across the sofa so she was sat next to me to emphasise her point. "I just wanted to set things straight. Yesterday was just... nostalgia. It was a mistake, it was my fault and I didn't want you to get the wrong end of the stick." She went to touch my arm, then thought better of it. "It's just been weird seeing you again after all this time, knowing what I felt about you back then, but never acting. It's been a little confusing."

The room swayed around me and I had to put out a hand to steady myself. What she'd felt about me? A small ball of vomit worked its way up my windpipe, but I swallowed it down, wincing.

"What do you mean, how you felt?" I paused. "How did you feel back then?"

Nicola looked up into the air and sighed. Then she gave a wry laugh, before focusing her gaze back on me. "Scared. Confused. Horny. In love." She said all of those things and never took her eyes off me for a second. "I couldn't put a name to any of it back then, but looking back, that's what it was."

"In love?" I could hardly believe my ears. She'd felt it too. Deep down, I knew she had.

She nodded, and took my hand. "Looking back, yes."

Her thumb moved slowly across my palm.

I breathed in sharply.

Nicola Sheen had been in love with me, and I had been in love with Nicola Sheen.

It was the sweetest and cruellest blow of them all.

And now it was too late.

I shook my head and gave a rueful smile. "But you ran. You just *ran*." I reached for her hand.

We both stared at her hand in mine. What might have happened? What might have become of us if we'd taken the path less travelled?

That was then, and back then, Nicola had chosen path B and run like the wind. Cut to today and we were at another junction. Which way were things going to go this time?

Her mouth closing in on mine told me the answer. Within seconds, her hot, firm body was pressing into mine and my pent up energy suddenly had somewhere to go. Then Nicola's tongue was back inside my mouth, but unlike yesterday's slow, sensual probing, this time, there was raw urgency about it. This was ten years of emotion and what-ifs pressing into me, asking questions that couldn't possibly be answered.

My body was responding to everything Nicola was doing — pressing, grinding, wanting. I'd gone into cruise control, my moral compass covered with a blanket, my mind gone fishing. This felt wrong, but oh so right. When Nicola Sheen's hand worked its way under my top and cupped my breast, I let out a groan of sexual frustration that was raw and unpolished. I was collapsing into her right there.

Encouraged, she undid the button on my trousers and slipped her hand inside.

I stopped breathing.

I couldn't let this happen — not this way. I wanted to sleep with Nicola Sheen more than she would ever know, but not like this, not a quickie on my sofa. And not when she was engaged to my friend. It was so tempting, but…

Her fingers were *so close*, and it took every ounce of self-control I had to grab her arm and pull away, even though my pelvis betrayed me and pushed forward.

She stopped and opened her eyes.

We froze in time, suspended together.

Another train rattled by outside, and to my left, I saw our Christmas tree lights watching, blinking in disbelief.

"I can't," I whispered. I didn't mean it, but it couldn't be any other way. "Not like this."

She crinkled her eyes, pain radiating from her. "I thought—"

I shook my head. "—Not like this," I repeated. "I can't do this with you now. You're not available."

She pulled her hand away and sat back on the sofa, breathing out in one long stream that I thought might never end.

We sat in silence for a few more seconds before Nicola sat forward and took a slug of her beer.

"This didn't go as I planned," she said, still breathing rapidly. She put down her beer.

"No?"

She shook her head and twisted to look at me. "No. My intention was to come over here and smooth things over. Not take it up a notch." She exhaled again before rubbing her hands together. "Like I said, nostalgia."

She turned and took another swig of her beer before jumping up, smoothing herself down and tucking herself in. "I better be going if I want to stay engaged," she said. She gave me a thin-lipped smile, but her gaze didn't falter.

"And is that what you want?" I had to know. I had no idea if Nicola Sheen was what I wanted, but I had to know whether or not she wanted me.

Nicola blinked and bit her lip, before nodding slowly.

"Absolutely," she said, looking away. "I'm marrying Melanie. I just — I wanted to apologise and then… this." Her gaze bounced around the room before settling back on me. "I'm sorry for yesterday, for today, for back then — for it all." She picked up her rucksack. "See you, Victoria."

But she didn't move.

I stood up. "Yeah, see you."

We stared.

And stared.

Nicola went to say something, then shook her head.

"I've got to go," she said. But her eyes told a different story as they dropped to my lips.

But this time, she did turn around and walk away.

Where Nicola Sheen was concerned, normal service had been resumed.

***

I was stood at the kitchen counter trying to put my thoughts in order when I heard Holly's key in the door.

Shit. Nicola had only just left, and my emotions were strewn across the floor. I was too disoriented by everything that had happened, and I wasn't sure I could explain it to Holly even if I tried.

Holly was frowning when she came into the lounge. She took one look at me and began shaking her head. "I was hoping that just bumping into Nicola on the stairs was a coincidence. Perhaps she knows someone else in the block, perhaps her sister lives here? But I know that look. You did it, didn't you? You just fulfilled your teenage fantasy and had sex with your childhood sweetheart."

I said nothing — it was all I could do to hang on to the kitchen counter and not collapse in a heap.

"Why do this? Why complicate your life?" Holly plucked a beer from the fridge and sat on the sofa. "Are you coming to sit down or are you going to just stand there?" She sounded hurt, wounded.

"Not if you're just going to lecture me. It's really not what I need right now."

A gamut of emotions passed across Holly's face before she settled on something between concerned friend and pissed off. "I'll try not to. I'll try to keep an open mind." She paused, then held up three fingers in a Girl Guide salute. "I promise."

Promise is what had got me into this mess in the first place.

I walked over and slumped on to the sofa, falling into Holly who had no choice but to acquiesce. She might still be boiling mad at me, but when push came to shove, I was still her best friend.

"So what happened?" Holly began stroking my hair. "And just so you know, this is not in the roadmap for getting a girlfriend by Christmas. The caveat I wasn't aware I needed to point out was that the girl in question had to be single, and not engaged to be married." I heard her take a swig of her beer and I burrowed my head deeper into her shoulder.

"I know," I mumbled. "But we didn't have sex. We nearly did, but we didn't."

Holly's body went taut. "You didn't?" She was holding her breath.

I pushed myself into a sitting position and ground the heels of both my hands into my eyes. When I refocused, my vision still wasn't totally clear.

I shook my head. "Nope."

Her hand rubbed my back as she exhaled. "Well that's good. That's really good. But what was she doing here?"

I turned to Holly and explained what happened the day before in the bridal shop.

She was silent the whole way through, her face turning a shade of grey when I relayed the kissing part.

"It was kinda left up in the air so she texted and asked to come over." I shrugged. "It seemed the right thing to do, to draw a line under it."

"And how did that plan go?" Despite her tone, Holly's face remained blank.

Guilt rose up in me, threatening to drown me. "Not so well," I said, shaking my head.

Holly's face softened. "Did you really think it would go any other way? You kissed her yesterday, there was unfinished business, she comes over to your flat where you have some privacy…" Holly held out her hands, palms upturned. "It's textbook 101 seduction technique."

"I was not seduced," I pouted.

Holly smiled, shaking her head. "No you weren't," she said. "But how did you leave it?"

Now it was my turn to shrug. "We kissed, but we're done — I know that's as far as it can go. And that's not just because she's getting married, it's also because we're different people now." I shook my head again. "Just sometimes I forget that, and she's still Nicola Sheen who I loved. So please don't be angry with me — I can't deal with it tonight."

Holly paused. "I'm not angry, I'm just looking out for you. I don't trust Nicola as far as I can throw her. Never have."

She pulled me into a hug and I let her.

Then I remembered Holly was supposed to be on a date tonight.

"Hang on — what are you doing home anyway?" I sat up again. "What happened to your date?"

Now it was Holly's turn to sigh. "She didn't show. No warning, nothing. So this dating game? It's not all it's cracked up to be." She swigged her beer.

My heart broke for Holly now — she was golden, she didn't deserve that. "I'm sorry about your date, and not just because she was called Ivy." I reached for Holly's hand and squeezed it.

Holly looked into my eyes and shrugged. "It's okay," she said. "She was hardly my soulmate."

14

Sunday December 11th

Sunday morning dawned and if there was ever a day I needed a distraction, it was today. As I lay on my bed and tried to clamber over the traffic clogging up my mind, I tried to identify what I was feeling. Confused, disappointed, and like I wanted to get in a time machine and erase the last few days.

I could still feel Nicola's hand on me, nearly in me.

It would have been so easy.

However, this Nicola Sheen wasn't the one I'd been in love with. She had a child. She was divorced. And she was engaged, yet thought it fine to come on to me three weeks before her wedding.

So yes, while yesterday had been the culmination of a dream, I had a feeling it might also serve as a reminder that you should never go back. It was a motto I lived by when it came to bad customer service in every other area of my life, so why didn't I apply it to my love life?

Ten minutes later, Holly burst into my room just as I was opening the next Advent calendar door and popping a chocolate Christmas pudding into my mouth. There was something very decadent about eating chocolate so early in the morning.

"Get up — we're going out," she announced.

"We are?" I asked, through a mouthful of chocolate.

Holly swept her dark hair from her eyes and nodded. "Yep — executive decision. You've been stupid and I've been stood up within a week, which is a new record even for me. So we're going out to do something fun to take our minds off it. Something Christmassy, guaranteed to put a smile on your face."

She grabbed my arm and pulled me up, marching me down the hallway and into the bathroom. "Get in the shower and get clean — we're leaving in half an hour and I've booked us an hour of ice-skating at Somerset House."

I did as I was told.

Forty minutes later, we were sat on a Tube, clutching cups of hot coffee, eyes wide open. Holly's knee was jiggling beside me — she always had a lot of nervous energy fizzing around her system and this was the usual out.

"Excited?" she asked, slapping my leg. "Ice, Christmas tunes, skating and mulled wine — this has to be right up there in your Christmas must-dos, doesn't it?"

I smiled, despite myself. "It is. I was going to buy some ice-skating tickets for me and a date if things went well.

However, I don't seem to have been able to limp to that stage quite yet, so this is perfect. I get to do it with my best friend instead."

Holly smiled at me and took my hand in hers. "Today we're each other's date, okay? And let's face it, we've both already gone one better than our last — I'm single and you showed up. We're winning at life already!"

I laughed. I had to agree.

Somerset House was an old Tudor palace on the Thames, a building that never failed to impress. During the winter its large courtyard became a Christmas grotto with its ice rink as the central play. As soon as I saw it strung with festive lights and pumping out 'Merry Christmas Everyone' through the surrounding speakers, happy seasonal endorphins flooded my body.

Maybe Holly was right, maybe this was the perfect thing to take my mind off my problems.

There was only five minutes till we were on the ice, so we exchanged our shoes for skates, then edged out slowly on to the freshly polished ice, currently a creamy, unblemished square all ready to be signed by us. Most people didn't need a second invitation once the klaxon blasted, apart from the ten per cent who'd forgotten how to skate since their childhood and were now doomed to spend the next hour gingerly crawling around the rink's edges, or flat on their bum.

Just as I thought that, I heard the first thump of the day, and turned to see a man in his 40s flailing on the ice.

"That's gotta hurt," Holly said.

We skated off side by side around the rink, pushing off from the left and then the right, just as my instructor had taught me all those years ago.

"How you feeling?" Holly asked as we were nearly cut up by one of the ice marshals on a mission.

"Surreal." I grabbed Holly's arm as I wobbled.

"Okay?"

I nodded. "Just getting my balance." I paused. "I'm okay. I feel a bit guilty and annoyed with myself and her. However you paint this, it hardly makes her the catch of the century."

We skated on in silence for a few more seconds. "And did I tell you the other thing?"

Holly didn't turn to me. "There's more?"

"She's got a kid and she still lives with her parents."

"Whoa!" Holly slowed her skates and coasted into the hoardings, and I followed.

"A child? How did she get a child?"

"Did you miss that class at school?"

Holly gave me a look.

"She was married before." I said. "To a man."

Holly spluttered. "She's already been married? I mean, to a man is neither here nor there, but this is her second wedding?" She whistled through her teeth. "She clearly loves getting married."

"Apparently."

We were silent for a moment as the mass of skaters

shuffled and sailed past us in clockwise order, a blur of smiles, furrowed brows and woolly hats.

Then, as Mariah Carey's 'All I Want For Christmas Is You' began to pump through the speakers, Holly took my hand and dragged me back into the throng. "We haven't come here to stand on the sidelines and process — we've come to skate!"

I screamed as Holly's yank nearly put me on the ice, but I styled it out. Within seconds, we were gliding and the steady concentration the skating required really was proving just the distraction I needed.

That is, until five minutes later when I was clattered from behind, a skater clearly losing their balance and sliding into the back of me, leaving me nowhere to go but down. My bum hit the ice with a deadening thud that reverberated up my body. Damn, the ice was cold.

I immediately went to spring back up, but my skates weren't being so obliging and I fell again. Crack. Ouch. A hand came into view which I presumed was Holly's, so I took it gratefully and pulled myself up to a standing position, arms outstretched to secure my balance.

"Thanks, Holly," I said until my eyes fell on my saviour.

It was Nicola Sheen.

I turned around and saw Holly was helping Melanie to her feet, Melanie wiping down the back of her jeans which were now wet through.

"What are you doing here?" I was whispering for no good reason.

"Same as you — skating." Nicola's tone was deadpan, her expression vanilla. She didn't seem freaked at all that we were meeting the day after we nearly had sex, and that pissed me off royally. Did none of this mean anything to her?

"Really? You never mentioned it last night." If she was stalking me, I wasn't amused.

Nicola baulked and my insides flared red.

"It never really came up, did it?" she said. Now her tone was gritty, like this was all my fault.

Thankfully, Holly butted in. "Great to see you guys, but now Melanie's in one piece, we're going to get in some more skating." She offered her hand to me while fixing me with a solid stare. "Shall we?"

I glanced at Nicola, then at Melanie, before taking Holly's hand. I was grateful to her for offering an easy escape, although still piqued at Nicola's casual brush-off. I wasn't sure how we were meant to act with each other now either, but hostile was not the first option that sprang to mind.

Holly's grip was like a vice as we skated off, faster than before. I didn't like to point out to her that no matter how fast we went, we'd still just be going round and round in a circle.

The ice rink was suddenly a metaphor for life.

"I cannot believe they're here too," I said, glancing at Holly.

"I can't believe you were talking to her. And that

she helped you up first before her own fiancée. She's got some nerve."

Holly tightened her grip again and I narrowly missed crashing into a stranded child.

"Hey, slow down," I said. "You're hurting my hand and I don't like going this fast."

"I just wanted to get away from them — I was trying to do you a favour."

I squeezed her hand and pulled her back — I needed to make her see things from my perspective.

Holly reluctantly slowed.

"I appreciate that, but you have to let me deal with this my way. This is my mess, my situation, not yours."

"I just don't want her treating you like shit, like always." Holly's face softened. "You don't deserve that."

I saw something in her eyes then, but I couldn't quite place it. Protection? Chivalry? Love? A merry-go-round of terms whizzed in my brain, but I brushed them aside and pulled her gently into the hoardings. I couldn't deal with anything else on top of the fact that Nicola was here right now.

"Nice of you to say, but racing around an ice rink isn't going to affect that either way. Just relax and let's try to enjoy this, like you said." Just as the words came out of my mouth, Nicola and Melanie stuttered past us, Melanie grimacing, Nicola looking less than pleased.

"We can definitely skate better than them," Holly said.

"Very true." My mind flicked back through my Nicola

album and landed on a memory from my youth — Nicola and I skating around our local ice rink, arm in arm. It was romantic back then, and now Nicola was trying to be romantic with Melanie. The morning after she'd come round to seduce me. Anger bubbled up my body.

"I'm going back in." I skated off, not waiting for Holly and not looking back. I was trapped and angry and not in the right space to be on an ice rink, that was for sure. I scanned the area. Where were they? I glided past three teenage boys in a line holding hands, sure to topple backwards at any moment. Then a small child skating backwards without a care in the world. Then a young couple holding hands, skating together, in love.

And then I saw them. Melanie had found her centre of balance and her body language was far better than it had been a few minutes earlier — she was getting the hang of it, but still grasping Nicola's arm. She wobbled slightly and Nicola put an arm around her waist. Then she leaned in and said something, and they both laughed.

And that's when I realised — they were one of the happy couples too. So what that we'd snogged in the last 24 hours? It wasn't impacting on their day. That made me even more angry.

They were in my sights now, but I wasn't really sure of my plan. I wanted to disturb their happiness, get my own back. How dare Nicola be smiling and laughing. What about me? What about my happiness and my Christmas girlfriend quest? Nicola showing up had completely blown that out of the water, thrown me off my game. If she hadn't shown up, I'd surely have bagged a girlfriend by now, would have carried on dating.

But she'd proved a distraction.

Now I was going to be a distraction right back.

I revved forward, going left to avoid a woman in a red ski jacket, then right to skate around a weeping child on the floor, an ice marshal in attendance. They were so close, with their backs to me, still laughing. I could just clip the back of Nicola's heels and skate off like nothing happened, right? And once she went down, Melanie was sure to follow.

I was five feet away, ready to strike when I felt an arm on mine — Holly. She pushed me left, but in the process went right into the back of Nicola and Melanie. There was a yelp as they fell forward, a crack as all their bodies struck the ice, Holly on top of them, me gawping at the sight. I changed the direction of my skates and swooped in to help Holly.

Nicola was still on the floor, struggling to get up. "Did you do that on purpose? There was plenty of room around, why would you do that?"

Holly gripped my arm and clambered to her feet, wincing and holding her right knee. "Of course it wasn't on purpose — I was pushed and went into the back of you. I'm not an idiot."

"Could have fooled me," Nicola snapped, her expression souring by the second.

An ice marshal skated in to help Nicola up, then Melanie. When he was satisfied nobody needed hospital treatment, he skated off to his next casualties.

"I'm an idiot?" Holly said, wrinkling her forehead. "You really want to get into idiocy stakes right now? Because I think you'd win hands down, don't you?"

Oh shit. Please don't say anything. Please don't let this all blow up in my face now. Not when it's over. Not when I'm just coming to terms with it. Not when this isn't even what I want anymore.

I glanced at Holly who was grinding her teeth.

Nicola opened her mouth, went to say something, then closed it. She looked from me to Melanie, then back to Holly, then at the floor.

"What are you talking about?" Melanie asked Holly.

"Why don't you ask your fiancée," Holly said, her tone as hard as the ice we were standing on.

I couldn't take any more — this was all getting far too close to the truth and if it came out, there's no way Melanie would ever forgive me. I couldn't let that happen. I grabbed Holly's arm and squeezed it in an attempt to get her to shut up.

This wasn't really letting me sort out my own mess, now was it?

Melanie turned to Nicola. "What's she talking about, babe?"

Nicola shrugged in response. "I've no idea. I know she's your friend, but she seems a bit unhinged." Just then, a tall man in a blue jacket grabbed Melanie's arm as he went by, nearly taking her down. Nicola saved her, giving the guy a mouthful in the process.

"Unhinged? Holly is not unhinged. Holly is my best friend and looking out for me." I pointed at Nicola. "Something you've never done in your entire life." I was dimly aware we were getting stares on the ice now, but it was too late.

"Come on," I said, tugging Holly's arm. I was so over this. "Let's get out of here — I think I've had about as much drama as I can take."

"Hang on," Melanie said, grabbing my arm. "Why would Nicola be looking out for you?" Her tone was sharp.

"Maybe that's something you should ask Nicola," Holly said, taking my arm.

Her grip was firm, stopping me from saying anything else. As my skates slid me away to the safety of the ice hut, I risked a glance backwards, but Nicola wasn't looking my way. Instead, Melanie was remonstrating with her, her words hitting Nicola with machine gun rapidity.

Nicola could do nothing else but stand there and take it.

***

We were sitting in the plaza at Covent Garden sipping mulled wine, our breath freezing in front of our faces. I'd been looking forward to my aprés-skate drink in the ice rink bar, but Holly had rightly pointed out it was probably best to get as far away from there as possible.

So we'd made the five-minute walk to Covent Garden, and now we were sat at the end of the covered market, giant baubles hanging from its ceiling in a riot of festive colour, to our right a magician holding court in the midst of a bulging weekend crowd.

"So what's next today — are we going to try to bump into any more of your exes to spice up our Sunday?"

I didn't think Holly could ladle any more sarcasm on to that comment if she tried — it was almost drowned in it. She was smirking at me, but there was exasperation in her eyes too.

"I thought mulled wine, followed by more mulled wine," I said, taking a sip and smiling as it warmed my insides. "What was Nicola like today? Playing the dutiful girlfriend and fiancée. Made my blood boil."

"I could tell," Holly said. "That's why I jumped in when I saw you about to take her out from behind."

"That really worked."

"At least I broke the speed you were going — I took most of that hit, so I'll be billing you when my knee swells to the size of a football, which it feels like it might have already." Holly leaned over and rubbed her knee through her jeans, which were slightly ripped.

"Sorry," I replied. "But you do have further to fall."

The magician in the black suit showed the crowd his empty hand, then shook his arm and produced an orange silk handkerchief followed by a mass of coloured beads. Muted applause.

"You know you have to walk away now, don't you? Leave Nicola to sort this out — no more meeting up just the two of you. I think I could tell you where that would end."

I said nothing, just continued to stare at the magician who was now tapping a black box with a white-tipped wand.

A bit of magic in my life would go down rather well right about now.

"Tori?"

I turned to Holly and sighed. "I know." I was resigned. "I know all that, but it's hard to walk away when there's a row of what-ifs hanging over the outcome. What if we'd got together at 16? What if her getting together with Melanie was just so that we could meet again?"

"What if she's a cheat with a child and no home?"

"I know," I replied.

"She's not the same person she was at school. Or maybe she is, and that's the point."

"I know." I was getting agitated, even though I agreed with what Holly was saying. I absolutely did, it was just my feelings hadn't quite caught up with my brain. "But sometimes, it's difficult to walk away from someone even if they're unsuitable and emotionally all over the place. Do you get what I mean?" My eyes bore into Holly — I wanted her to understand.

She looked away and took a deep breath. "You don't know everything about me, Tori. You think you do, but you don't."

15

Monday December 12th

The following day at work and I was feeling guilty about yesterday and my temporary bout of insanity. It hadn't been fair to Holly or to Nicola. However, my attention was temporarily diverted by the toaster being on fire. Again. This time it wasn't my fault though.

I held my breath as the fire engine drew up, but Nicola wasn't on board. I couldn't decide if I was relieved or disappointed. Whichever, I knew I needed to see her again, to really sort things out — we needed proper closure, yesterday had made that clear. I couldn't turn into Tonya Harding every time I saw her with Melanie.

So at lunchtime, having asked one of the firefighters which station they were deployed from, I hopped on a bus and was there within 15 minutes — she'd worked just around the corner all this time. It would be funny if I could locate my sense of humour.

The station looked deserted apart from two fire

engines, which were gleaming on the forecourt. I walked in and spotted a man in uniform bending over some equipment. When I asked about Nicola, he looked me up and down, then pointed towards an office tucked away on the right-hand side.

She was the boss, so of course she had her own office.

I walked over, took a deep breath, smoothed down my coat and knocked on the door.

"Come in!"

I did as I was told.

Nicola's face fell when she saw me. "Victoria." She tapped a pen on her desk and fidgeted in her chair. "What are you doing here?"

"I thought I should come and sort things out." I paused. "Can I have a seat?"

She motioned to the free one on the other side of her desk. "Please." She tugged at her shirt collar and cleared her throat. "How are you?" Her eyes searched mine.

I screwed up my face. "Not brilliant." I decided to take the bull by the horns — I didn't have much time, so small talk wasn't on the cards.

Besides, Nicola hated small talk.

"I wasn't really sure what to do after the other night. And then we saw each other skating yesterday... I don't want that to happen again." My throat was clogging up with emotion, but my voice was coming out clean and clear. Decisive, almost.

"Me neither," Nicola replied, not looking me in the

eye now. "Saturday was a mistake. And yesterday at the ice rink didn't help. Tell Holly thanks for mowing me down."

I didn't move my gaze from hers. "She wasn't to blame." It was a statement, not one to be messed with. "Anyway, I can't stay long, I've got a meeting in an hour. I just want to know we're okay, seeing as we will be bumping into each other again. The lesbian scene isn't that big, no matter what anyone tells you." I was relying on Nicola for a solid answer.

She shrugged, which wasn't the best response for the current situation. "We're going to have to be, aren't we? I can't walk away from Melanie. She's good for me. I'm not going to mess this one up too."

I frowned. "You shouldn't marry someone because you think you owe them something."

"I know." Nicola paused, before fixing me with those eyes again. "But we're solid. She's dependable."

"Really?"

"Yes, really. And me and you... the other night — it was like we were just picking up where we left off. It's too hard. I've always had feelings for you, but they mess with my head."

I gulped and tears needled the back of my eyes. Every time she said something like that, it took me back to teenage Nicola. The one I'd been in love with.

There was a knock on the door and it opened swiftly. A man with red hair walked in, but stopped when he saw me. "Sorry guv, didn't realise you had company."

"Can you give me five and I'll be with you?" she told him, holding up her hand.

If the man noticed Nicola's watery eyes, he gave nothing away.

"Sure," he said, smiling at me as he backed out of the office.

Nicola stood up and walked around the desk, leaning on it in front of me before taking my hands in hers. "I have to go — I've got a briefing to do."

A tear trickled down my cheek. I didn't know why. I hadn't come here to pursue anything with Nicola, but I didn't want this moment to end. I was fighting with my teenage self and my normally rational present self.

"I don't want this to be the end of us — even as friends." I paused, searching my mind for something to say. Nicola's hands were hot around mine. "Do you still love country music?"

She nodded.

"Then come to the Dixie Chicks with me." Even as I said it, I knew it was wrong. But it was out of my mouth before I could control what I was saying.

She furrowed her brow. "You've got tickets? They sold out in minutes." She paused. "Remember when we were meant to go to that concert all those years ago?"

I nodded, putting an image of Holly out of my mind, even though every fibre of my being was screaming at me to take the offer back. But I wasn't operating via normal me — I was operating via 16-year-old me. "I do. But we never got there that time, did we?"

Nicola narrowed her eyes. "Things got in the way."

"Boys got in the way."

She nodded, then cast her eyes to the ground, before returning them back up to me. "I'd love to come with you." She paused, before tilting her head. "You give off very mixed signals, you know that?"

I nodded, not trusting myself to say anything else.

"I've got to go. Drop me a text with the details?"

I nodded and got up, already cursing myself as I left. Why had I said that?

I was so going to hell.

***

It was now less than two weeks to Christmas, and I was no closer to getting a girlfriend. If anything, my plan for a Christmas girlfriend had shaken up my world and thrown a whole load of trouble my way in the past couple of weeks. On top of that, I'd promised the Dixie Chicks tickets to Nicola in a moment of stupidity, and now I was regretting that enormously. My stomach lurched as I thought about breaking the news to Holly. It could wait. I decided to go to bed as I'd probably done enough damage in the world for one day.

I brushed my teeth, spitting out blood as I did — it represented the world I was living in. Messy. When I got into bed, sighing with relief as the covers soothed my skin, I stared at the ceiling and thought about my dad. He was probably looking down at me and shaking his head right now. Christmas was meant to be all about lightness and giving, but I knew that with the Dixie Chicks tickets, I'd taken the giving a step too far. I had to make that right before Holly found out.

"What would you do, Dad?" I asked out loud, before stilling my breathing and waiting for an answer.

Nothing came.

Perhaps my dad was too busy stringing up Christmas lights and drinking mulled wine with the angels — sounded about right.

But I knew he wouldn't be happy with what was going on. I needed to just walk away from Nicola completely, no good could come of it. And then Holly would be happy too.

Holly. *Oh god, the tickets.*

I pulled the covers up over my head and willed sleep to take me away.

Perhaps everything would seem a lot clearer in the morning.

16

Tuesday December 13th

Holly and I were meeting in the drinks department at Selfridges to buy some overly expensive alcohol for our annual Christmas soirée, usually held the weekend before Christmas. Holly always had a party around that time to celebrate her birthday, which fell on Christmas Day — hence her festive name.

Last year we'd bought some fancy type of eggnog, specially imported from the USA and it was demolished within the hour. This year there was just as much festive bling on offer, with specially made sloe gin, Christmas-spiced rum and festive fizz, along with swag like specially printed Christmas glasses and cocktail shakers. In truth, I wanted to buy the whole shop, but I knew Holly wouldn't go for that, being far more practical and prudent than me.

Holly arrived ten minutes late, giving me a hug and complaining about the Tube. I shook it off — Holly was ten minutes late wherever she went, it was her ritual.

She was dressed in a smart grey suit with those slip-on shoes with tassels that were so in vogue right now — with her height, Holly never needed to add heels. She'd had her hair cut recently and it hung down over her eyes, short at the back. As usual, Holly looked like she'd been expressly delivered from a catwalk show to come shopping with her vertically challenged friend. It was a role I was well used to playing.

"Have you found anything?" Holly rubbed her hands together, her green eyes twinkling. "I'm surprised you haven't bought the shop yet."

"I only *thought* about buying the whole shop, there's a world of difference."

Holly chuckled, before picking up a bottle of Smirnoff Gold. "This would be a good talking point." She shook the spirit and the gold leaf danced around the liquid.

"Bit noughties," I said. "What about this?" I held up a bottle of bright blue liquid, which had a reindeer head fixed around its cap so that when poured, it looked as though Rudolph was vomiting up your drink.

Holly screwed up her face. "I don't think so — blue drinks are never good news."

But within five minutes we'd struck gold: mince pie liqueur. "Mix it with rum to make mince pie martinis," Holly read from the label. "That'll do nicely."

We bought three bottles before heading off to the Selfridges' Christmas department to buy a new ornament for the flat — also now one of our Christmas traditions.

The department was vast, stacked floor to ceiling with shiny Christmas objects and decorations, all vying to be the one to adorn your home. Honestly, I could have happily moved in here for the festive period, pretending I was in the movie *Elf* or similar. This Christmas department represented a world where everything was simple, and the biggest decision you had to make was whether or not to eat a candy cane or a mince pie for breakfast.

After 20 minutes breathing in the filtered essence of pine cone, we settled on an uber contemporary snow-covered branch as our new ornament, replete with a red-breasted robin. It was going to look great on our lounge wall.

Next up on the list was family shopping. I always bought my mum a selection of treats from the Selfridges' food hall, along with something woollen. This year, Holly chose to follow suit. We bagged our mothers identical grey cashmere jumpers and hoped they'd never meet wearing them, along with a selection of nuts, chocolates and weird cheese.

Which just left buying for each other so we agreed to meet in the champagne bar in an hour — we had to have bought our presents by then. We called this our annual Christmas dash — you could pre-plan, but you could not pre-buy.

I knew where I was headed: bags. Holly needed a new one that fitted her laptop as well as her daily life — she'd been telling me so for weeks now. I'd done my research, which meant I found the perfect bag within 20 minutes and had it gift-wrapped on the spot. I was pleased with my choice. The bag was cherry-red leather with tassels to match Holly's shoes, had a wealth of pockets and leather so smooth, you could fall asleep on it.

***

Holly was waiting in the champagne bar with a grin on her face when I arrived, two glasses of fresh bubbles on the table along with a bowl of green olives. Most of the other tables were full of shoppers relaxing after spending their cash too, drinking wine and champagne, as well as eating some of the bar's tapas offerings.

"All done?" Holly asked. She smiled and it lit up her whole face — she looked extra-gorgeous tonight.

I stashed the presents under the table, dropping my handbag on to the back of the chair.

"Yep and you're going to love what I bought you," I said.

"I don't doubt it." Holly sipped her drink, before rubbing her hands together. "So I was thinking, tonight could be the start of our Christmas extravaganza."

I tilted my head. "Our Christmas what?"

Holly scratched her forehead and stretched her legs out so they snaked down the side of my chair. "If your Christmas girlfriend quest is really over, then maybe we should just throw ourselves into Christmas, just the two of us and our plans. What do you think?"

Guilt crept up my face. Turns out guilt was coloured red.

"What's the matter?" Holly narrowed her eyes. "This is right up your street, but you're not jumping up and down." She paused, then sat back in her chair. "You feeling okay?"

I licked my lips before shaking my head. "I'm fine, just need some food. This champagne has gone straight to my stomach. The Christmas extravaganza sounds perfect. But what does it involve?"

Holly grinned and was engaged once more. "Tonight, we do dinner under the twinkly Christmas lights. Then tomorrow we watch a Christmas movie, your choice, and I'll pretend to be amazed when you choose *Elf*. Then there's the party, Dixie Chicks, my birthday — we're all set really!"

My face fell. Dixie Chicks.

I put my finger in the air and pursed my lips, then took a large gulp of my champagne. Then another. It was nearly all gone.

"We better get you some food sharpish if this is your drinking mood," Holly said with a smile.

"About the Dixie Chicks."

Holly's face formed a question mark. "What about them?" She withdrew her legs and sat up. "You did get the tickets, right?"

I nodded. "I did." More nodding. "But I might have promised them to somebody else."

Holly looked confused and rightly so.

"What?" She looked like she wanted to scrub out her ears, like she couldn't possibly have heard right.

Only, she had.

I downed the rest of my drink and grimaced. I really was a terrible person.

"The thing is, I saw Nicola yesterday. And things were fraught. I know she loves country music, and it just came out. I wanted to make her feel better, make the situation better, so it just slipped out. I'm so sorry. But I can take it back, and we can still go. I've been meaning to. I just haven't had the time."

Holly didn't say anything. She just breathed deep gulps of air, then stood up, shaking her head. Her jacket was on before any words spilled from her mouth.

"Nicola. I might have known Nicola Sheen would be involved somewhere. You just can't help yourself, can you? Tori Hammond, whirlwind central. Do you just like drama? Because if you do, you're doing a stellar job."

It was like she'd just punched me in the face, and frankly, I wouldn't have blamed her if she had. Holly was being horrible to me, and while I knew I deserved it, it didn't make it hurt any less. This was Holly. We were more than just friends. We were a unit. We were... I couldn't find the words to say what we were.

"Holly." I stood up and put my hand on her arm.

She threw it off abruptly. "Don't try to brush this one off, Tor, it's not going to work. You know how much I wanted to go to the Dixie Chicks — *you know*. Yet you still did this. Incredible. Well, I hope you really enjoy those tickets. I hope they play all the hits, and I hope you don't feel one ounce of guilt when they play our song — the one we always sing." She picked up all her bags and brushed past me. "I'm going home. I suggest you don't do the same for a while as I don't want to look at your face any longer than I have to tonight. Call your girlfriend, I'm sure she'll come and meet you."

"She's not my girlfriend," I said, but Holly was already out the door and heading down the stairs to ground level.

I sat back down and ordered another glass of champagne, tapping the bag with Holly's present.

She'd calm down eventually. She always did.

"It'll all be fine," I said out loud to nobody.

But this time, I wasn't sure it would be. This time, I'd overstepped the mark and what made it worse was I could have covered it up and never told her. But it just slipped out. Now everything was ruined and it was all my fault. If they were giving out gold medals for bad friends, I was about to take the title by some distance.

I stared at my fresh glass of champagne, at the bubbles fizzing to the top, but I couldn't embrace their jollity.

My mood was sinking so fast, I feared I might fall through the floor at any moment.

17

Thursday December 15th

I arrived home from work exhausted from the week so far. I'd texted Nicola to tell her the Dixie Chicks tickets were off after my disastrous shopping trip with Holly, but she hadn't texted me back. I guessed my friendship with Nicola wasn't going to go anywhere fast now, but after the turmoil of the previous couple of weeks, I was fine with that.

I didn't know what I'd been thinking in Nicola's office that day — not much, apart from wanting to please younger me. But my current life was far more important than my past, and I was going to try to be a better person. Now I just had to tell Holly and let her know that our friendship meant the world to me. That she meant the world to me. But that all hinged on her being happy to talk to me, and that might be the trickier sell.

I'd also spoken to my mum the previous evening and told her the whole sorry tale. She was now coming into town on Saturday and meeting me for lunch on the pretext of some Christmas shopping. She hadn't said much in response apart from dropping in the odd sympathetic platitude, but I expected she was coming to tell me much the same as Holly had on Tuesday. Ever since then, Holly had been courteously polite to me when we'd crossed paths in the morning, but tonight was the first time we'd be home together since Dixie-gate.

I picked up the post from the mailbox in the reception area and got the lift to the fifth floor, punching the button and waiting for it to move. There was a bank statement for Holly, some junk mail from a catalogue for me, plus a handwritten envelope addressed to both of us. I was intrigued.

I ripped open the hand-written envelope just as the lift doors sprung open. I hitched my bag up my shoulder, unlocked our front door and threw my keys down on the shelf in the hallway — they scratched the wall as they landed. Damn. Dropping my bag, I pulled the contents of the envelope free and stopped still, blinking rapidly as I read.

'Melanie Taylor and Nicola Sheen are pleased to announce their marriage and would love you to be there to celebrate their special day on Saturday, December 31st…'

I stopped and stared.

So she was going ahead with it — that was a good thing. She was engaged after all, and the logical thing for people to do when they were engaged was to get married.

Nicola Sheen was getting married.

I'd known that all along. And I didn't have an 'It Should Have Been Me' feeling about it.

The feeling washing through my bones was 10 per cent betrayal but 90 per cent relief. Nicola Sheen was in the past and that's where she should have stayed all along. Still, my movements were heavy as I put the invite on top of my keys and turned away from it. Then I hung up my coat, went through to my bedroom and collapsed on my bed.

Ten minutes later, I heard the front door slam, which shook me from my stasis. I heaved my body upwards, peeled the clothes from my body, applied more soothing, comforting homeware of tracksuit bottoms and my favourite yellow T-shirt, and then headed into the lounge. The invite was no longer on the shelf as I passed.

When Holly heard me shuffle into the lounge, she turned and walked over, stopping just before she got to me.

"You okay?" she asked.

I nodded, but bit my lip. "I'm fine."

"I saw the invite."

I gave her a weak smile. "Really, I'm fine."

But she gave me a hug anyway, because that's what friends do, and I let her. Sure, we were still fighting, but some things trumped fights.

After a few moments, I untangled myself from Holly, walked over to the fridge and pulled out one of her beers. "Want one?"

She nodded.

I uncapped two and handed her one.

"You're drinking beer?" she asked.

I shrugged. "I've decided to be a different version of me from today, one who puts myself and my friends first. And maybe Tori 2.0 drinks beer, who knows?" I took a swig and tasted the familiar bitter taste. I couldn't quite keep the wince from my face. "I might get used to it."

We both sat on either end of the sofa, a train rattling by as we did so.

"Have you heard from Nicola?" Holly held up the invite.

I shook my head. "She's been very silent this week. Now I know why — other things to do." I puffed out my cheeks and blew out a long breath. "I don't know why I feel a teensy bit betrayed, but I do." I drank some more beer. "I'm more relieved than anything else, but my teenage self is a bit sad. It's always nice to be the chosen one, even if it was never going to work in the end."

Holly looked away before answering. "Very true." She paused. "But you're always the chosen one with me. Even though sometimes you really don't deserve it."

I grimaced. "I know. I'm sorry about everything, I really am. I've told Nicola she's not going now, and I hope we can go to the concert as planned. It's what I always wanted. They were always your tickets."

Holly spluttered. "Not what you said on Tuesday." Her tone was disbelieving, then her face sagged. "Giving those tickets away like you did really hurt."

Holly's words cut me to the core. Never in a million years had I meant to hurt Holly. But I had. She'd ripped down my defences and exposed me for the terrible friend I was. I wanted to make it better, make Holly see it was one mistake and that our friendship was way stronger. It had to be, I couldn't cope without it.

I took her hand in mine before speaking. "I don't know what else to say apart from sorry again — you've no idea how sorry I am. Hurting you was the last thing I wanted to do." I hoped Holly believed me, but I had a feeling it might take more than mere words.

"I know you are," she said, shaking her head and dropping my hand.

A cool breeze of my own making washed over me.

"But you're so infuriating. You just do things and don't think about the consequences. I know spontaneity is all the rage these days, but sometimes, so is a calm, measured approach to life."

I sighed. "I know. But you do that much better than me. It's not my strong point."

"I'm not sure how long that excuse is going to wash, Tori."

I frowned. I didn't like the sound of that. "What do you mean?" My voice was quiet.

"I mean you have to grow up and get real. Saying you're no good at something is not an excuse to then make the same mistake again and again. If you're no good at something, work at getting better at it. Especially if the consequence of not doing so is hurting the people closest to you."

I let the words settle on my skin and seep into my bloodstream before replying. "I promise I'll try. I know giving the tickets to Nicola was a mistake. I knew it as soon as it came out of my mouth. But once it was out there, it was done." I shrugged.

"And then what happened?"

"Sorry?"

"Then what happened?" Holly sat forward, looking at me.

"I don't get you."

She laughed softly. "I think that's the point I'm trying to make."

Her words were slightly barbed, but she was smiling. At least that was something.

Holly shook her head again. "I'm saying that after you made the mistake — and you knew it was a mistake — you did nothing. You hid. You hoped that someone else would come along and sort your mess out for you. But guess what? Nobody did. Your mistakes are for you to deal with.

"You did the same with Nicola. You never put a stop to it, even though you knew it was going nowhere. You did it with Amy too — she was the one who called it off. Everybody else has the same issues to deal with, and they do. You need to start dealing with your life rather than running away from it."

I said nothing, just looked around the room. I knew I deserved this, but it didn't make it any easier to take.

But Holly wasn't finished. "Running away creates drama and you love drama. But you don't need it, that's what you don't realise. You're fine as you are. You can be the star of your own life, you don't need other people to define you. It was the same with your Christmas girlfriend quest. You couldn't just date like everyone else, you had to have a theme, a deadline — more drama."

I glanced over at Holly, taking in her words. Was she right? Did I court drama wherever I went? My life had certainly always had its fair share. Maybe she had a point. Maybe I did do it to myself.

"You should come out for lunch with my mum on Saturday," I said glumly.

Holly looked at me quizzically. "I should?"

I nodded. "Yep. She's given me this speech before too, or similar. You could tell me in stereo."

Holly smiled. "No, we'll just tag-team. I'll do today, she can do Saturday."

I gave her a weak smile. "You make me sound like such a moron. An emotionally defunct moron." I put my head in my hands. "Am I that bad?"

Holly was silent for a few seconds too long.

I burrowed my head deeper.

"You're just you, Tori, I know you and I love you." She paused, as I looked up. "But that doesn't mean you can't make better choices and make a change. See what I mean?"

I sighed and nodded. It was nothing I hadn't heard before. And maybe now I was reaching my late 20s, the cuteness factor was wearing off somewhat. But Holly still loved me, that was something at least.

"I do," I said. "And I will totally try. You have my word. Is that good enough?" I searched Holly's face for an answer. She waited a few seconds before replying.

"It is if you mean it," she said.

I bit my lip again. "I really do."

"Then I'll look forward to Tori 2.0. She sounds like an interesting, sassy woman." Then she smiled at me, a proper full face smile this time, and when she did, I realised how much Holly's approval meant to me.

I stared at the train that was passing by the window, waiting for the noise to die down before replying.

"So am I forgiven?"

Holly shook her head, then smiled. "You're forgiven. You're an idiot, but you're forgiven."

I smiled back. "I was going to give the tickets to you all along, honest. Nicola doesn't deserve them — you do."

She waved her hand. "Let's leave Nicola out of this from now on, shall we? We're going to the Dixie Chicks, just like we planned. Our Christmas extravaganza is back on. What do you say?"

A wave of warmth washed over me as I held up my beer for her to clink. "Here's to us and our Christmas extravaganza."

"Here's to it," Holly replied, tapping her beer bottle to mine.

She held my gaze and my stomach did a backflip.

Honestly, my emotions were all over the place this Christmas.

18

Friday December 16th

I opened two days of my Advent calendar and ate the chocolate for breakfast, then made my way to the office. The weather had turned grey and exceedingly damp. This morning, the heavens had opened and as I'd walked from the Tube, water was racing along the gutters, the torrential downpour slapping the concrete like a scorned lover. I'd run the gauntlet of trying not to get in the way of a giant wave from a passing car, and I'd just about managed it.

Now, I was in my office kitchen, grinding beans for my first coffee of the day. Surprisingly, I'd slept fine last night, but my dreams knew something was up. In it, I'd been walking up the aisle on my wedding day when I woke up, sweating and confused. I was pretty sure the woman waiting for me was Nicola Sheen, but I couldn't be certain — she seemed taller than her from the back. Now, a couple of hours later, I still had that odd, wary feeling you get when you have a dream that's far too close to real life. I preferred my dreams to be abstract and bizarre rather than based in reality — like that dream where I'd married Kristen Stewart. After that one, I'd been smiling for the whole day.

Sal walked into the kitchen looking exactly as I felt — tired and like she wanted to still be asleep.

"Morning No. 1," she said. "No arson plans today?"

I shook my head with a smile. "None this morning, but maybe later if I'm bored."

Sal laughed and slotted two slices of bread into the toaster before opening the fridge to grab the butter.

"Make sure you watch the toast, though," I said. "That toaster is dodgy, mark my words."

"A bad workman always blames his tools," Sal replied.

I finished making my coffee and raised an eyebrow at her. "Just make sure you watch it."

I walked through to my desk and opened my emails — only 35 new messages overnight, not too daunting. I smiled at a picture of Holly and me from last summer that I had as my screen saver — it was just after we'd done a skydive and we had our arms around each other, grinning into the camera. It always made me smile, plus it reminded me I was capable of anything if I put my mind to it. Outside, the rain was still skating off the dark grey roof tiles and a crunch of thunder made me turn my head, quickly followed by a shard of lightning.

I was on my third sip of coffee when I smelt the smoke, and just raising the mug to my mouth when Sal ran past me the other way. Too late — the fire alarm was already blaring.

"Sorry!" Sal was standing in the kitchen doorway, her face clenched. "Looks like we're going to have to evacuate again. I promise to buy a new toaster today." She caught my eye and gave me a tight-lipped smile.

There was a collective grumble as people winced at the noise of the fire alarm, then gathered their coats and bags before trooping down the stairs, brollies in hand. On the pavement outside the water jumped up, hitting calves and shins, while windscreen wipers worked overtime as we huddled in the doorway of the local supermarket.

Everyone else was willing the fire department to get here quick and sort this out, but I wasn't one of them. I wanted to be nowhere near the fire engines when they arrived.

"Not you this time," office manager Maureen said to me.

"Apparently not," I replied, fixing her with a death stare. Possibly a slight over-reaction on my part, but Maureen should know when to shut up. It wasn't one of her qualities.

Five minutes later and the fire engines turned up. Nicola Sheen and her colleagues got out, fire gear on and ready to tackle the toaster again. She looked around, searching out Maureen. When her eyes spied the high-vis jacket, Nicola began walking towards us.

"Here we go." Maureen let out a sigh and stepped into the rain, umbrella up. I've no idea why, but I followed her.

When Nicola saw me next to Maureen, she stopped. I could see the battle of professional versus personal playing out in her mind, but eventually professional won the day. She came to a halt inches from me, her face giving nothing away.

"Morning, Maureen," she said, as if this was just any other day. Nicola's vision was set to tunnel mode, and Maureen was the only person at the end.

"Nicola," Maureen replied. "I'm so sorry, it's our damn toaster again."

"It's pretty bad when you're on first-name terms with me." Nicola glanced at me. "You again?"

Was that a smirk on her face? If it was, I really wanted to wipe it off. "No, actually," I said. "Believe me, you're the last person I wanted to see this morning." I paused. "How are the wedding plans?"

Nicola flinched, but then regained her composure, turning her focus back to Maureen.

"You're getting married?" Maureen said. "How wonderful! When's the happy day?"

"Less than two weeks, isn't it, Nicola?" I closed my eyes as I said it. Why couldn't I just shut my mouth?

Maureen looked from me, to Nicola, and back. "You two know each other?"

"Old school friends." Nicola kicked a stone on the pavement as she said it.

Another crunch of thunder interrupted our joyous conversation. I moved as central as I could get under my umbrella, whereas Nicola just stood and stared, water cascading off her shiny helmet, her uniform seemingly making her indifferent to the weather conditions.

"Let's try to get this over with as quickly as possible, shall we?" Nicola said, glancing at me again.

I presumed she was talking about the fire alarm.

"Right you are," Maureen replied.

Nicola turned on her heel and Maureen scuttled after her, disappearing into the building without a single look back towards me. The wind had picked up now and the rain was slanting horizontally into my body, my umbrella not much help at all.

I ran towards the building and took shelter in the reception area, along with the other fire marshals from the other floors. My umbrella dripped silently at my side and the air was filled with the scent of wet tarmac and gently steaming bodies, damp and bothered from the inconvenience. Sal was nowhere to be seen — was she hiding under her desk eating the offending toast?

When Nicola and Maureen came back down the stairs five minutes later, Maureen was clutching a clipboard and nodding to Nicola, who was being followed by a colleague I recognised from their previous visit.

Maureen rolled her eyes as she passed me. "Off to round up the troops," she said. The other fire wardens slipped off to do the same, and with Nicola's work colleague out the door as well, it was just me and her. However, this morning, even in her uniform, Nicola did not spell desire. Rather, she spelled Trouble with a capital T.

"I hope the wedding goes well." My voice was flat.

Nicola scrunched up her face. "Really?"

I gave her a tight-lipped smile. "Really."

She smiled grimly. "I'm sorry about everything. I was just confused and got a bit nostalgic. But I'm marrying Melanie. I can't let her down."

"A great basis for a marriage," I said.

"I've heard of worse," Nicola replied, folding her arms across her chest. "Anyway, you and me, we'd never have worked. Not with Holly in the picture." Nicola fixed me with her eyes as she said it.

"What's Holly got to do with anything?" I was genuinely perplexed.

She angled her head. "Really, Tori? It was always there at school, you know that. But now? You two should just bite the bullet and get it over with."

I shook my head. "Stop trying to deflect the situation. Me and Holly are friends, that's all. You're the one who kissed me—"

"—And you pushed me away? I don't think so."

We both stood glaring at each other, daring the other to take it further.

Nicola blinked first. "Face it, Tori. We had unfinished business. Now it's finished. You can get on with your life and I can get on with mine. Although I've taken you off the wedding list. I assume you're not coming?"

My hand was on the move before I could stop it. I reached out and slapped Nicola across the face. That was for my present self, as well as my 16-year-old self. The sound as my palm connected with her cheek echoed around the building's reception, and I heard a gasp behind us. I gasped internally too — far from being satisfying, I just felt a bit sick.

We both turned to see Maureen standing there, jaw hanging open, along with half the rest of the building behind her. I wasn't sure how long they'd been standing there, but I was pretty sure they'd seen me slapping Nicola, the first time I'd ever done such a thing in my whole life. I stared down at my hand, which was shaking, and then up at Nicola who was clutching her cheek.

I still couldn't believe I'd just done that.

After a few moments, she puffed out her cheeks and shook herself down. "I'll take that as a no then," she said.

With that, she whipped around and signed Maureen's admin sheet. "I'll be sending one of my officers round next week to check all your devices so you'd better get new ones. Otherwise, I'll be issuing a fine. Clear?"

Maureen nodded meekly, then Nicola walked out of the door and out of my life. Again. But this time, I had a feeling it was for good. I felt the cloak of closure settle on my shoulders, and it fitted perfectly.

Once she'd gone, the rest of the office workers began streaming up the stairs, leaving me standing, shell-shocked.

Maureen made her way over to me, concern etched on her face. "Everything okay?"

I exhaled loudly. "It will be," I said, giving her what I hoped was a reassuring smile. "And don't worry, I only slap people I'm really mad at." My hand was still stinging.

"Remind me not to get on the wrong side of you in the future, then," she replied.

19

Saturday December 17th

I met my mum just after one o'clock under the Swiss cuckoo clock in Leicester Square, which wasn't the best place to meet someone on the penultimate Saturday before Christmas. Half of London was there, prowling around, looking for wildly inappropriate goods to spend their money on. I hated rushed Christmas shopping, so was glad I'd got all of mine out of the way already.

My mum was a mass of floaty material and beads as always — I often joked this must be the learned dress code in professor school. Her hair was shoulder-length and she'd dyed it recently so it was the colour of honey. She was wearing her comfortable shopping shoes from Marks & Spencer and was already clutching at least three shopping bags, as I knew she would be. My mum was an early riser and she liked to hit the shops as soon as possible to beat the crowds. "If you don't get there till lunchtime, you've lost already," she always said. Which was the main reason why we rarely went shopping together.

"Alright, kiddo." She gave me a chaste kiss on the cheek. "I would hug you, but I'll save that till we're sitting down and I can drop these bags." As she said it, a tourist ran past and almost knocked Mum over. "Shall we get out of here before I get trampled?"

I took one of her bags before indicating over my shoulder and she followed me. Within five minutes, we were in Soho and in one of my favourite restaurants, which did a fabulous set lunch for prices that didn't break the bank.

"Lunch is on me," I said, pulling out my chair.

"I knew I had a daughter for a reason." Mum gave me the promised hug, which nearly knocked the wind out of me before slotting herself and her shopping into and under the chair.

We ordered from a very smiley waiter, and once the wine had been poured, we relaxed.

"So you are coming home next week?" Mum took one of the bits of French bread and smothered it with butter.

"Course. Unless I get a better offer."

Mum spluttered. "Charming. You're going to leave me with your gran and Aunt Ellen? That shows a huge lack of Christmas spirit, if you don't mind me saying. Especially from one who loves Christmas so much."

I smiled. "I'm joking — you know I wouldn't miss it. How is Gran?"

"Gran is great — the usual. And Ellen's back and itching to go away again already, so no change there either."

My mum's mother was faring well, still strong and independent at the age of 75. Her older sister Ellen was also giving old age two fingers at every opportunity, having just returned from a safari in South Africa. I loved spending time with both of them and hoped I was as funny and healthy at their age. Plus, they were both huge red wine fans, so we spent a large chunk of Christmas Day trying new bottles — hence they tended to be a little boozy. Which was exactly the way my gran planned it, so she could then clean up at poker in the evening. She always seemed to miraculously sober up at that point.

"So what better offer are you waiting for?" Mum asked, as the food was brought to the table. French classic beef bourguignon for her, coq au vin for me.

I shook my head. "I was joking — I'll be there."

Mum chewed her mouthful before replying. "Nothing to do with Nicola Sheen?"

I cast my eyes down. "No. We ran into each other yesterday and that is done and dusted." I relayed the story to Mum and she clicked her tongue in response, an annoying habit I knew well. It meant she had more to say, but she was holding back for now.

"And what did Holly have to say?"

"I didn't see her last night — she was out with work people."

"What's she doing for Christmas?" Mum took a sip of her wine, but kept her eyes focused on me.

"The usual," I replied. "Some time with her dad, some time with her mum and nobody's happy. Always makes me value our Christmases even more when I hear about hers."

Mum chewed slowly. "She should come to ours — the more the merrier."

"I'm sure she'd jump at the chance," I said, waving my knife in the air. "But you know, family politics."

"Well, the offer's there if she changes her mind." Mum raised an eyebrow, then carried on eating.

"What was that for?" I asked.

"Hmmm?"

"That," I said, mimicking her movement. "The eyebrow raise, the 'wait and see' look."

Mum shrugged. "I've no idea what you're on about." She ate some more food and put her fork down. "So tell me about some of these dates you went on. They sound like a hoot. Especially the one where you fell asleep on the loo."

***

After the Dixie Chicks tickets and all the grief I'd put her through, I knew I owed Holly big time. So I texted to say I'd meet her at home that night. After I left my mum with our Christmas plans ringing in my ears, I stopped off at Marks & Spencer and bought one of their meal deals, ready to grovel to Holly. And if that didn't work, I bought extra chocolate and wine for added back-up. After all, one bottle of wine was never enough in these situations.

When I got home, the flat was dark and quiet — Holly wasn't home yet. I switched the Christmas tree lights to a cool mood setting, then flicked on the others before adding some candles to the mix. Then I selected a chilled playlist on Spotify and set all the food out ready on the counter. I wanted Holly to know I'd made an effort, even if actually cooking the food was a little beyond my skillset.

The next thing I knew, Holly was gently shaking me awake — wine at lunchtime always made me sleepy.

"Hey," she said, her hand on my shoulder. "Are you trying to burn the place down? Because I really don't think we need Nicola Sheen coming over again this evening, do you?"

I rubbed my eyes and sat up. "Agreed, we definitely don't want that." I yawned and stretched both arms above my head, my groan timed with a train rumbling by outside. "I must have fallen asleep."

"No shit, Sherlock," Holly replied. She looked around. "Is this all for me?"

I nodded. "I was trying to make it..." The word romantic popped into my head, but that didn't seem right. Or did it? "Relaxing." Definitely a better choice of word.

"I'm honoured." Holly paused. "Let me dump my bags and I'll be right out."

I stood up, brushing myself down in an attempt to shake the sleep from my system. I checked my watch —

I'd been out for nearly an hour. Shit, I really could have burned the place down. Note to self: must take steps to try not to become a serial arsonist.

I put the oven on and was piercing film lids when Holly reappeared. She was wearing jeans and a distressed black T-shirt that sat just so on her body as if she'd been dressed by Tyra Banks. That's what comes of being so tall — clothes just work on you. For Holly, the biggest gripe was women's tops being too short and not covering her stomach. As she often pointed out, crop tops were never a good look on anyone, let alone accidental versions.

"So you're cooking me dinner to apologise for being a crap friend, is that right?" Holly was leaning against the counter and grinning at me. "And when I say cooking, I mean it in the loosest sense of the word," she added.

I glanced at her, my knife poised above a container of tenderstem broccoli. "Hey, nothing screams 'I'm sorry!' like an M&S meal deal. Fact." I waved the knife around. "Look it up on the internet, it'll totally say so."

Holly crossed her arms, an amused smile playing on her lips. "So what's for dinner, MasterChef?"

"Well," I said, tapping the black plastic containers. "For mains, we've got duck breast fillets with soy, honey and ginger and I bought some chips as an extra side."

"An extra side? You're really pushing the boat out." Holly paused. "And what's for dessert? Have you ordered burlesque dancers followed by high-class escorts and cocaine?"

I clicked my fingers together. "Damn, I knew there was something I forgot — gimme two ticks and I'll go order the cocaine."

Holly laughed as I put the food in the oven.

"Should take about 20 minutes," I said. "Beer to start?"

"Beer would be perfect." She paused. "Did you buy those too?"

"No, you did." I passed her a beer and we sat on the sofa, facing each other.

"So you're keeping up this beer drinking thing then?"

I nodded, taking a swig. "See, I didn't even wince then, did I?" There was jubilation in my voice.

"You did not," Holly replied. "Well done, I think?" She paused. "How's your mum?"

I nodded. "Really good. Excited about Christmas and she's got me *even more* excited about it now, too."

Holly pulled a face. "Glad someone is — we're rapidly approaching one of the most anti-climactic weeks of my year. Christmas and my birthday in one, and every year my parents choose to celebrate it by arguing. Happy holidays!" Holly bent a leg up on the sofa and hugged it to her chest.

I wanted to make it all better for her, but knew I couldn't.

"My mum invited you to ours — you've done it before, remember? Maybe you should do it this year too? Reclaim Christmas and your birthday and make them your own."

Holly gave me a tepid smile. "A nice plan, but I don't think I'd ever hear the end of it if I did that, and then I'd just have to deal with warring parents on the phone rather than in my face."

"But wouldn't that be better?"

Holly shrugged. "They'd find a way to ruin it, whatever."

"Just think about it — for me?" I pulled my extra-special pout, the one Holly could never turn down.

She put up her hand to shield her face. "Not the pout!" she said. "Save me from the pout!" She paused. "I'll think about it."

"Thank you," I replied. "But staying serious for a minute, I do want to say sorry again — about everything. I was an idiot and we're worth so much more than any love interest in my life. We've been through so much together, and that matters." A train rumbled past and I waited before continuing.

"So tonight is my very humble and really not quite grand enough way of starting to say sorry. But this is only the beginning. For a start, I'm paying for the Dixie Chicks tickets, taking you out to dinner beforehand, and will also buy you another night out, all expenses paid. You deserve it."

Holly's face registered surprise, then she curled her mouth up into a smile that reached her eyes. I hoped I was fulfilling my part of the bargain, of taking responsibility for my mistakes.

"To us," I said, holding up my bottle. "Whatever

life throws at us, let's always stay friends and have each other's back, no matter what."

Holly raised her beer bottle back towards mine. "To us," she said, fixing me with her gaze. "I've always had your back, and I always will."

My stomach dropped as she looked into my eyes. I recognised the feeling in the pit of my stomach, but it wasn't a feeling I was used to having with Holly.

Excitement. Attraction. Desire.

I opened my eyes wide as the shock of the revelation jolted my heart, but I managed to control my breathing and style it out. However, when I gazed at Holly's face, I was pretty sure I saw just what I was feeling reflected right back at me.

Holy batshit. Was this what Nicola had meant when she'd said we could never have a relationship with Holly around? And was this what all my mum's raised eyebrows and unspoken questions had been about too? Did Holly like me *like that*? It was far too many questions for my brain to cope with. As I stared at Holly, my clit twitched and I closed my eyes.

Then I shot up from the sofa, ignoring the static in the air and the fluttering in my chest. If I was about to have a heart attack, this was not the best time for it. I'd thought tonight, of all nights, was going to be complication-free, but apparently not.

"I'm just going to check the dinner." I scooted over to the oven, avoiding looking at Holly for fear I might blurt something out or give something away — what, I wasn't quite sure.

"You only just put it in."

She was right, of course.

"Yeah, but I was just thinking that perhaps I should have seasoned the duck."

When I turned, my gaze fell on Holly and my vision went blurry. It was as if I'd been seeing her one way my whole life, and now, someone had flipped a switch and Holly was a femme fatale. In grey furry slippers. Her short, dark hair flopped adorably on to her forehead, a lot less fussy than it would have been had we been going out tonight. Her T-shirt now clung to all the right places and I blushed as my gaze stopped momentarily on Holly's breasts before looking away quickly.

"Do you think I should season the duck?" I opened the cupboard to look for seasoning. Then I looked back to Holly. "What does seasoning mean, exactly? I've never known that, it always seems a bit general, doesn't it?" I was babbling, which was strangely reassuring. It meant I was reacting as I normally did when I liked someone.

But now Holly was putting down her beer and walking over to me, and I wasn't sure I could take such close proximity now that the cat was out of the bag and my heart was telling me its deepest, darkest secrets. I might implode if she came within three feet of me.

When I'd thought about getting together with Nicola, there had always been something holding me back, always been a missing piece of the jigsaw puzzle. Something beyond the fact she was a relative stranger with personal baggage galore.

Standing here in front of Holly, there were no questions, no what-ifs. The puzzle was complete and everything slotted into place. I knew everything there was to know about Holly and I liked it all. I'd been so busy running around and creating drama, I hadn't stopped to see what was right in front of me. And what was right in front of me was so much more than an image on a dating app. Holly was a 3D person and she was everything I was looking for.

However, the prospect of acting on that piece of the puzzle was absolutely terrifying, because what if it went wrong? I risked losing everything. Our friendship, my home, my security — and my love for Holly. Because I did love her, I always had as a friend. But turning it into something more? That was too much to comprehend.

"What do you mean, what's seasoning?" Holly asked.

What was she talking about? My mind drew a blank. Seasoning? I'd been hit with a startling new revelation in my life, and Holly was talking about seasoning?

But no, hang on, I'd been talking about seasoning, hadn't I? The rest had been an internal dialogue with just me participating. Right, I remembered now. Seasoning.

I blinked.

Holly furrowed her brow. "You okay? You're acting very strangely."

The heat from her body was leaping on to mine and I felt dizzy. Weak. I had to focus.

"Fine," I said. I buried my head back inside the cupboard so she couldn't see the panic written in pink highlighter on my face or the fear currently lodged squarely in my chest and throat. What if I vomited all over her? I really shouldn't have had that tiramisu dessert with my mum at lunchtime.

"So which seasoning did you say?" My head was still in the cupboard. "I've got Cajun, nutmeg, coriander, mixed herbs." I twisted the small pots of herbs to read their labels.

Holly touched my arm lightly. "Tori, come out of the cupboard."

But her touch on my arm made me leap into the air. In doing so, I managed to knock a couple of the pots of herbs from the shelf, and they bounced off the kitchen counter and on to the floor. Luckily, they were made of plastic so they didn't smash. I turned to pick them up, but Holly was already on her haunches.

I dropped down to the floor myself to help her out, as one of the herbs had flipped open and a mass of dried oregano was now littering the kitchen floor.

Holly grabbed the dustpan and brush from the under-sink cupboard and as she bent back down, we came face to face with each other. And when I looked at her, something changed. My brain flipped to romance mode, and everywhere I looked, my vision was misted and objects airbrushed. It was as if my mind had just installed a photo editor and was trying out every happy filter possible. Right now, my whole world was set to Sunshine and Yellow Glow.

I stared at Holly.

She stared at me.

I dropped my gaze to the spilled herbs, but when I looked back up, she hadn't taken her eyes off me. My heart rate revved like a motorcycle engine and blood zipped around my veins. Was I about to pass out or about to kiss my best friend of a million years? I couldn't be certain which way this one was going to go.

But it turned out that Holly was sure, so the passing out option was bypassed.

Before I could react, Holly's lips were pressing into mine, soft, firm and beery. She didn't try to rush, she just let her lips linger and caress, stroking across mine, taking her time. The effects of her kiss shot through my body with utmost force, causing my fingers and toes to curl, holding on for dear life. It was sublime and it was happening to me. *With Holly*.

I sunk into the kiss with my best friend, and magic pulsed in the air around us. The trains wound down, light increased and there was a ringing in my ears, but it was a happy sound. Our lips slipped over each other like they'd been made to measure, whispering a secret to each other they'd been bursting to tell. But the secret was out now, and there was no way of putting it back.

I've no way of knowing how long we kissed, but eventually Holly gently pulled away. She held me by the top of my arm, a smile playing on her lips. She went to say something, her eyes locked on mine, but then she just pressed her lips back on to mine lightly before pulling back again.

When I opened my eyes, the world felt brighter, shinier, more defined. I'd kissed a lot of women before, but I'd never been kissed like Holly had just kissed me. This was so much more than just a kiss.

"Your lips feel pretty good," she said before kissing me again.

"So do yours." I reapplied my lips to hers and I felt it right where I was meant to.

This shit was getting real, but I wasn't scared. Rather, I wanted to clutch our possibilities, because right now, they seemed limitless. Especially when my lips were on hers and nothing seemed impossible.

I only stopped kissing when we nearly toppled over, both of us still down on our haunches, the herbs still on the floor.

When I looked at Holly, I was stuck for words. None of them seemed adequate for what had just happened.

"So this is… interesting," I said finally. "Kissing — we don't normally do that."

Holly smiled, then shook her head. "No, we don't."

"And when we do, we do it squatting on our kitchen floor."

Holly laughed. "It's a first for me. For you too?"

I rubbed a hand up and down her arm. "Yep. I'm a kitchen floor kissing virgin."

I stood upright and offered a hand to Holly.

She took it, hauled herself upright and cracked her head on the open cupboard door. Hard. She was immediately back down on the floor again.

"Shit, that sounded like it hurt. You okay?" I was on my knees beside Holly, who was sat on the kitchen floor, clutching her head and swearing under her breath. "Holly?"

She groaned in response and I stroked her arm.

"Can you see if it's bleeding?" She was still trying to catch her breath.

I peeled her hand away, noticing for the first time how long and slender her fingers were. Which of course then sent a shudder down my entire body, and I had to blink to remember what I was doing: looking at Holly's head and checking she wasn't bleeding to death.

"I can't see any blood," I said. "But let's get you up and over to the couch."

She nodded slowly and made it to the sofa where she laid out, wincing. I brought her a bag of frozen peas and she held it against her head. Then I sat at the bottom of the sofa with her feet touching me, assessing her body, the body of my future lover I had no doubt.

I'd never slept with anyone so much taller than me. Holly's body was slim and went on for days, and

I shuddered again as I imagined touching her for the first time, holding her breasts, kissing her neck. I blinked.

I must stop having amorous thoughts while the object of my affection might be concussed.

"How you feeling?"

Holly peeked out from under the frozen peas. "I'll live," she said. "But I'm more than a little upset that when I finally get to kiss you — and believe me, that's something I've been wanting to do for weeks now — I then nearly knock myself out and end up like this."

She'd been wanting to kiss me for weeks? This was news. But when I looked at Holly, holding her head, I decided to revisit that later.

"You don't need to worry," I said. "Just relax for now till you feel better. This is you and me, there's no hurry. We've got all the time in the world." I got up and walked over to Holly, and her eyes sparkled like diamonds. I leaned down and kissed her slowly, cupping her face and slipping my tongue inside her mouth.

She groaned lightly.

I didn't stop for a couple of minutes. I put all my effort into it, everything I was feeling in that moment. Right there, Holly and I were connected in a way I could never have imagined the day before. It's funny what life throws at you, isn't it? When I pulled back, my head was spinning, and Holly was looking at me like I'd just given her the world.

"Fucking hell, Tori. Where did you learn to kiss like that?"

My cheeks reddened. "I teach it at the Lesbian Skills Centre, didn't I tell you? That's where I've secretly been going most weeks, not actually spin class as I've been telling you. It was a top secret mission."

Holly grinned, then remembered she was in pain and frowned.

"You okay?" I dropped to my knees by her side. "Should I get you a headache pill or something?"

Holly stared at me, her pupils large. "I'm only thinking about one thing right now, but that might make my head explode." She grinned at me. "Let's just see how we go with dinner and wine, and then we'll take it from there, okay?"

I nodded, then pushed myself upright before swooping to kiss Holly one more time. "And can I just say, this is one of the few times I'll be able to say I leaned down and kissed you, so I'm taking advantage of it."

Holly beamed at me. "I've told you before — when you're this tall, you have to spend half your life horizontal just so your partner can have a fair crack at kissing you. It's something I've learned to live with."

And then Holly winked at me.

I went weak at the knees.

Literally.

***

Dinner was a surprising success — even without the seasoning. Turns out, these ready-made dishes already have all the seasoning they need. Holly also told me over dinner that seasoning meant salt and pepper.

"Why don't they just say that then?"

She wasn't able to give me a satisfactory reply.

We ate the duck at the dining table with Holly gingerly touching her head every few minutes.

"It feels like there should be a dent in my skull."

I confirmed there was no dent, nor was there a torrent of blood pouring down her face. She eventually believed me and began to relax. However, I understood her dilemma. After our unexpected snogging, relaxing over a good meal and acting normally wasn't as easy as it sounded. Tonight was turning out to be anything but normal.

My senses were still dialled up to the maximum setting, so every time Holly moved, spoke or even glanced at me, I was preparing for her to say something profound, something life altering. Something that would make my heart soar, or make my heart sink. Like that it had all been a mistake, and we should just eat this dinner, forget it ever happened and move on.

But she didn't.

Instead, she chatted about how she was dreading Christmas, how good the food was, how weird her head felt.

"You might be concussed. I listened to a podcast the other day about it. If you feel sick, that's a key sign."

Holly gave me a look. "Why were you listening to a podcast on concussion? Did you have a premonition?"

I returned her look.

"Or you could have poisoned me with your food. You're not exactly famed for your culinary skills."

"I'm serious. Dizziness, sickness, it's all part of it. So no more wine for you."

I topped up my glass, though.

Holly pouted. "I'd say tonight needs a little bit more wine, don't you?"

She had a point — I didn't want to tackle this without a little Dutch courage either. I topped up her glass.

We finished off with chocolate mousse, and then Holly beckoned me over.

I got up and arrived at her beckoning finger, and she pulled me into her lap.

"Now, where were we before the cupboard almost killed me?"

I gulped and shifted my gaze to Holly's mouth, taking in her smooth skin, her proud nose. I'd only ever been this close before when she was carrying me home drunk in our younger years — and we'd never even kissed then.

But now, I kissed her, and it felt like I'd been doing it all my life. Holly's mouth fitted mine perfectly, and her tongue when it slipped between my lips made my mind leap forward and think about what it might be like when it slipped between my other lips. And then my mind blanked out because it simply couldn't take the heat.

I pulled back and Holly stared at me.

"What did you stop for?" She was breathing heavily, her hand on my waist.

"Is it strange this feels both really weird, but also really right?" My breasts were sitting just below Holly's face and her attention wandered. I cupped her chin and made her look at me. "To my face, sweetheart," I said.

Holly stuck her tongue out at me.

I smiled. "I mean, kissing you — it feels amazing. But I'm a little shy about getting undressed in front of you. I've known you for years." I sighed and leaned my head back.

Holly gave me a squeeze. "It's only in your head it feels weird," she said. "Did you think it was going to be weird to kiss me?"

I thought about it. "A little."

"And was it?"

I shook my head. "Not one bit." I kissed her again to prove my point. "Nope," I said, shaking my head. "Still fine."

Holly grinned at me. "So don't you think the rest will follow suit? That it will just be fine?"

I bit my lip. "I suppose so. Should we get drunk just to make sure?"

Holly laughed. "No we shouldn't. I'd like to remember the first time I see you naked, the first time we have sex, wouldn't you?"

Boom! My whole body flushed with longing, and I was sure Holly would be able to hear the rush of my libido.

Holly frowned. "That okay to say? You're not one of those women who wants to wait till the fourth date are you?"

I grinned down at her. "Do I strike you as one of those women?"

"I hope not," Holly said. She pulled me in for another kiss, and this time, her hand kneaded my right breast.

And this time, I didn't stop to question it. This time, I just wanted more.

As if reading my mind, within moments, her fingers were undoing my shirt buttons, and her hand slipped inside, her thumb grazing my nipple.

I stopped breathing. If this was what was to come, I might die tonight, but I was going to die happy. I pulled back and stared down at Holly.

Without another word, she eased back my shirt and unclipped my bra.

We were both focused on my breasts now — Holly on them, me on Holly on them.

"I knew it," Holly said, kissing my left breast with utmost care.

At her touch, my clit swelled and I could feel myself getting wet — it was almost too much to bear. "What?" My voice was barely audible.

"Your breasts — they're amazing in clothes, but up close, they're mind-blowing."

I pulled her head closer to them, wanting to feel all of her mouth on me.

My breathing was ragged even before she took my nipple into her mouth, working it with her tongue. But afterwards? Then, my breath began to unravel through my body with every nip and suck. I might as well have been naked already, and that thought only drove me higher.

Holly had me just where she wanted me and just where I wanted her.

I leaned my head back. "Hols?"

No answer.

"Babe?"

She snapped her head back, her eyes intense. "Did you just call me babe?" A smile played on her lips.

"Er, yeah."

She grinned now. "You can definitely do that again." She reached up and pulled me down towards her, this time plunging her tongue into my mouth with raw need.

I felt a rush between my legs and the way Holly shifted underneath me, I knew she felt it too.

"You wanna—" I began

"—Yes," she said, shifting me off her lap. Then she was on her feet and dragging me towards the hallway, her chest heaving, her T-shirt low on her breasts.

But once she was in the hallway, she stopped abruptly before turning to me. "Your place or mine?"

I gave her what I hoped was a seductive smile and I think it worked as she didn't stop for an answer, kicking open the door to her room with her foot.

"Fuck it — we'll try my bed, then yours." Then Holly tugged me into her room, taking charge.

Within seconds, my loosened bra and shirt were

on the floor and she was standing and staring, shaking her head slowly.

"What?" I was suddenly shy, standing there half-naked.

But Holly just shook her head. "Nothing. You're just so… perfect. And your breasts are a work of art." She reached out and trailed a hand across them like I was a fragile masterpiece, price tag unimaginable. "Seriously, Tori."

I couldn't imagine a time when I felt more wanted, more sure. And I wanted this so badly too. I couldn't wait. I leaned forward and kissed Holly and then we were clinging to each other, steadying each other for what was to come.

Hunger radiated from Holly's stare as she began kissing my stomach, my sides, my breasts, my neck, a whirlwind of teeth, lips and tongue all over my skin. My entire body was alive and ready. Then Holly backed me into the bed and we tumbled on to it, me pulling off her T-shirt, and then her bra.

Seeing Holly like this for the first time felt anything but weird — it felt like this should be us, like this was totally right. She was so long and beautiful, like perfection with no end. I licked her small but perfectly formed breasts one at a time before turning to her nipples, my tongue circling velvet.

Holly groaned and squirmed beside me.

Inside, my body hummed like it never had before.

And then Holly was on top of me, shaking off my

jeans and pants, followed by her own. We were pulled together with an unstoppable force, and Holly's hands were everywhere, hardly giving me time to breathe. Just as I got over one sensation, another was lined up to crash over me. I could sense I was about to be overwhelmed and I welcomed it. There was nothing I wanted more.

And then Holly's hand was between my legs, her thigh pressing, pushing, wanting.

My breathing quickened. "Please," I begged. "I need to feel you inside me." My eyelids flickered open and I shared a brief moment with Holly. There was such tenderness in her gaze, she took my breath away.

And then she complied with my wishes, slipping one finger, then another inside me slowly, deliberately, never losing eye contact, raining kisses down on me.

My mind flipped into automatic pilot as the sheer bliss of the moment overtook me — Holly inside me, all around me, pressing me down, forcing me higher. Desire circled us like a hawk, going faster and faster, racing around the moment and leaving me dizzy.

Holly pulled me closer and I thrust my body into her, wanting more, knowing I could take everything she had to give.

She gave it to me.

We rocked together, never missing a beat, our rhythm our own and already a smash hit. I was filled to the brim, with yearning cascading from me, and I never wanted it to stop.

A couple more minutes and I was gripping her fingers, my body shaking, kissing her mouth, my body simply craving more. Then Holly brought her other hand into play, showing manual dexterity of the highest order. She brought a whole new meaning to the term 'being good with your hands'.

My orgasm started in my groin, then ripped through my body, exploding every muscle, pleasure throbbing through my being as Holly never let up, the maestro orchestrating the show. I was floored by her passion, sucker-punched by her lust. She sucked me into her vortex and I wanted to carry on spinning forever, never leave her, always be with her.

Moments later, I stilled her arm and she lay down beside me, kissing, stroking, loving, still inside me.

I didn't have any words. There was nothing to say. I just kissed her lips through the midst of my sex haze and hoped that I conveyed everything in that one movement.

I think she understood — she smiled, at least.

And then I kissed her again, and again, my lips and tongue not being able to get enough. I was soon working out that Holly was addictive, and I needed another fix. With a yearning to know what she felt like that was almost deafening, I got behind Holly, sliding between her legs, capturing her as my own. I had one thing on my mind and one thing alone — to give Holly an earth-shattering orgasm, one she'd remember for the rest of her life.

This was important — this was how we started.

As I moved inside her, she elicited a guttural groan that made the corners of my mouth turn upwards. She was slick with desire, offering herself up for me and I was lost in her body, in her world. She was a new terrain to navigate, but every corner was soft, smooth and sign-posted just for me. I snagged her neck then licked her back as I built a rhythm just for her, her name stamped right through it.

Within minutes, she was thrusting back into me, crying out my name at full volume, shuddering with desire. I took a snapshot with my mental camera of the first orgasm I ever gave Holly, my new love, the first of many to come.

Leaving her no time to recover, I rolled her over and licked my way down her stomach, my hair trailing across Holly's skin behind me. Then I went lower, tasting her lips, creating patterns with my tongue.

She cried out and thrust her hips.

I smiled and pulled her closer, pressing into her with my tongue before sucking her pulsing clit into my mouth.

Holly's moans swirled around my head and I felt invincible. When I slipped my fingers back in and spun my tongue around her clit, her body went into a state of frenzy. We were two people, but right then, we were one. I spun, flicked, spun, flicked. Holly came hard, gripping me, her orgasm rattling through her like one of the trains outside the window. When she was done, I crawled back up her long, slim body, placing kisses all the way up before lying on top of her and kissing the side of her neck.

We stared at each for a few moments, eyes locked, breathing rapid. We didn't say anything, but slow smiles spread across both our faces. Our first time had been divine, and the night was still young.

We lay panting in each other's arms, luxuriating in our post-orgasmic state. Then we sealed round one with a kiss.

We knew there would be plenty more to come.

20

Sunday December 18th

What had happened with Holly and I had come from left field, from a galaxy far, far away — but it just went to show that sometimes, straying into new orbits could be a very good thing. As I awoke the next morning with the winter sun streaming in through Holly's window, I couldn't have been happier. The air on this new planet tasted extra-sweet.

I stared at Holly, sleeping beside me, her hair sticking up at all angles. I was almost scared to touch her for fear of her vanishing as I woke up, all this just a dream. But it wasn't a dream, I knew that.

This was the gold-plated version of reality I'd been waiting for all along. This reality slotted into my life perfectly, like it had been specially commissioned. This new version of my life had a certain sheen, a solidity I wanted to show off to everyone.

I kissed Holly's cheek and she stirred, eventually opening an eye and looking up at me.

"Hey," she said.

"Hey yourself."

"Been awake long?" She rolled on to her back, yawning and stretching like a cat.

"Not really."

I scooted over the bed and into Holly's waiting arms, giving her a kiss before I settled on to her shoulder. "Morning, by the way."

Her hand found my arse and she gave it a squeeze. "Good morning to you."

I could hear the low thud of her heartbeat through her chest, and it was reassuring. A train rattled by outside the window.

"It's weird hearing the trains — I'm not used to it in my room," I said.

Holly kissed the top of my head. "Get used to it," she replied. "I plan on having you in my bed often."

I raised my head and gave her a lazy smile. "You do, huh?"

She gave a slight nod. "I do." She paused. "It's taken long enough already, so you owe me some time back."

Taken long enough? How long had Holly wanted me?

I rolled on top of her and she groaned as our bodies pressed together, naked flesh on naked flesh. Was there a better feeling in the world, especially with a new lover?

"How do you work that one out?" I asked.

"The time back thing?"

I nodded.

"Well," she said, her hands stroking up and down both sides of my body.

I wriggled and squealed.

"I did not know how ticklish you were, this is a new thing," Holly said. "Anyway, yes, time." She paused — she was choosing her words carefully. "Let's just say, you've come to my attention of late."

I gave her a look. "What does that mean?"

Holly thought for a moment, opened her mouth, then closed it.

"Whatever it is, spit it out," I said.

"I'm thinking."

"And we're friends. I'm not some random you picked up on the street." I wanted Holly to trust me. I kissed her to show how much I meant it. When I drew back, Holly looked dazed.

"You see, you ask me a question, then you do that. It's distracting."

"Sorry," I smiled, kissing her lightly again.

She cleared her throat. "Okay," she began. "You've always been attractive to me, but I never really thought of acting on it — we were friends, that's how things were."

I nodded. "I know, same here."

She smiled at that. "But then," she continued, wrapping her arms tighter around my back. "When you started on this crazy dating scheme, I started to get jealous of your dates. And then Nicola Sheen turned up and I wanted to punch her. That's not normal."

"You've always wanted to punch Nicola Sheen."

"True," Holly replied. "But I realised my jealousy had a motive, and I didn't want you ending up with her, even though you seemed hell bent on that scenario for quite a while."

"I was processing," I said, guilt bubbling up my body.

"Sure you were." Holly paused, giving me a peck on the lips before drawing back. "Then I went out on that date to try to take my mind off it, but it didn't work. I just kept thinking about you."

"But you arranged a second date."

Holly blushed. "I lied. There was no second date. I made it up."

I widened my eyes, feeling stupidly grateful that she'd lied. I didn't want there to be anyone else, especially not so recently. I wanted Holly and her affections all to myself.

"We all do stupid things." Holly raised an eyebrow at me.

She had a point, so I shut up. If I was feeling like that about her date, she must have been feeling wretched about Nicola Sheen.

"But once I knew why I was behaving like I was, I then had to work up the courage to act on it. There was a lot to think about." Holly grinned. "Luckily, the spilled herbs were the catalyst. I don't think I'm ever going to look at a pot of oregano in the same way ever again."

I brushed a strand of Holly's hair out of her eyes and kissed her. "Me neither," I said.

A few seconds passed.

"What about you?" she asked.

"Me?"

"Yeah — did you think about me like that?"

My breathing stilled. I had to think about how to answer this one — I didn't want to say the wrong thing, but I wanted to be honest.

"I'm a little slow on the uptake," I began.

"Judging on last night's performance, I disagree," Holly said, pressing her leg between mine.

I groaned. "What were you saying about distraction?"

"Right, yes," she said, not moving her leg.

I kissed her shoulder, then held her gaze. "You're gorgeous — that much everyone knows. You're tall, dark and handsome, but like you say, we were friends." I stopped to kiss her before continuing, wanting to wipe away the hesitation on her face.

"I don't know when that shifted exactly, but I'm glad it did. And I'm glad I knocked over the herbs. And I'm more than glad you kissed me, then fucked me like you did last night."

At last, Holly smiled back at me. "I can do it again now if you like."

I smiled back. "I was hoping you would." Another kiss.

She licked her lips. "So no regrets? You haven't woken up wanting to run back to your own bed?"

I shook my head. If she thought I was having any regrets about what we'd just shared, she was a mad woman. Last night had been one of the most intoxicating of my life and I wasn't about to walk away from that in a hurry.

"Only if you're coming with me," I replied.

21

Monday December 19th

The following Monday I was in town shopping after work. Holly was out with clients tonight, so we were having a night apart. Ever since Saturday, we hadn't spent much of our spare time out of bed, let alone apart. I let a slow, sultry smile invade my face as I strolled through the perfume department at Selfridges, running the gauntlet of the perfume sprayers.

I got on to the escalator and rode up to the Christmas department. I was still amazed Holly and I had happened, still newly thrilled every time I thought about it. I never expected to end up in bed with my best friend, but now it had happened, it seemed like the most obvious thing in the world. Why had nobody else pointed this out before?

That very morning, I'd taken myself off the dating app I was on, as had Holly. That was another plus point of dating your best friend — there was an inherent trust already there. When Holly told me she was deleting her profile, I had no question she was going to do just that. Not simply say that for my benefit and then do nothing of the sort, as I'd known plenty of others do before. This, too, was something I was going to have to get used to — being able to trust my girlfriend completely.

To celebrate us getting together, I'd decided we needed a new Christmas ornament. Something romantic, something that would put a bookmark in the story of our lives to say this was the Christmas where everything changed. The year when I set out to get a girlfriend for Christmas, but it didn't exactly turn out as I expected.

The Christmas department was pumping out its usual pine cone aroma, and everywhere you looked, there was fake snow, tinsel, shiny displays and candy canes galore. To my right, a full-size Santa welcomed me in with a broad smile, and to my left, a mini winter-wonderland had been constructed, replete with a snow-covered steam train winding its way through the white-frosted hills.

After 15 minutes of browsing and singing along to Bing Crosby's 'White Christmas' and Elton John's 'Step Into Christmas', I stumbled on exactly what I was looking for — a knitted Christmas pudding with the words 'Our First Christmas' embroidered on it. It was understated and cute, and not too brash to scare Holly off. I was pretty sure it would take more than a single decoration, but I still had to tread carefully. I'd never been Holly's girlfriend before, after all.

I was walking over to the cash desk when I spotted

her out of the corner of my eye. Melanie Taylor. I changed the direction I was walking and veered left, behind a giant Christmas tree. I wasn't up to dealing with Melanie yet, I didn't want anything to break into my happy Holly bubble.

However, when Melanie appeared at my side ten seconds later, it appeared she was not having similar thoughts. I tried to give her a fake smile, but it probably came off as a grimace.

Melanie's face didn't alter, despite mine going through a gamut of emotions.

"Tori," she said, her eyes steely. Did she know? If this was going to be a showdown, please don't let it be here. I did not want one of my all-time favourite places scarred with the memory of a Melanie Taylor meltdown. I'd seen them before.

"Hey," I replied, putting far too much forced jollity into my voice. I picked up a nearby wind-up Santa just for something to hold on to. I was expecting a bumpy ride from here on in.

"How are you?" I winced, waiting for the answer.

Melanie scowled at me. "I'm okay, considering."

I swallowed down. "Considering?" There was a lightness to my tone — I didn't want to reveal anything I didn't need to, so if I could get away with keeping this superficial and fluffy, that was my intention.

"Really?" Melanie's tone, however, had turned scratchy. "You're going to go the innocent route? If I was going to act on what I've been thinking about you over the past few days, I should be kicking your head in right now."

Panic alarms whirred in my head and tension seized my body. Melanie was considering beating me up in the Selfridges' Christmas department? I didn't know much, but I was fairly sure that contravened some sacred bond, some rich pot of Christmas spirit that needed to be tended and stirred regularly. Melanie was planning to contaminate the pot and knee me in the face in the process. I always said she was a bit bonkers. I gripped the wind-up Santa and turned its key nervously.

Melanie took a step towards me.

I wound the key even tighter and took two steps backwards.

"I knew there was something up between you two the first time I saw you together at that restaurant where you were eating that pitiful meal for one."

I could smell Melanie's breath on my face, and it had more than a whiff of crazy. I cast my mind back to that fateful evening that seemed so long ago now, with so much happening in the interim.

"You two were all 'we're just old friends from school'." She put the final part in air quotes with her fingers, before shaking her head. "When did that change? When did you sleep with my fiancée? And were you planning on telling me before the wedding or after?"

My mouth fell open and all my blood rushed to my cheeks. "We didn't sleep together."

I put down the wind-up Santa on the display unit next to me and he immediately began walking, shaking some small maracas as a tinny rendition of 'Jingle Bells' blared out of the top of his head. I blushed redder still, and we both watched in horror as Santa made it to the end of the first verse before toppling off the edge of the unit. I picked it up and set it back down again, and Santa immediately resumed where he'd left off, shaking and singing for all he was worth.

Melanie shot a hand out and laid Santa on his back, but his legs kept kicking, his maracas kept shaking. She picked up a nearby Christmas cushion and suffocated Santa. The tune became a mumble and Melanie turned her gaze back on me.

"Why are you lying?"

I shook my head vigorously. "I didn't... We didn't. We stopped before anything happened."

Melanie let out a sharp bark of laughter. "And that's meant to make me feel better?"

I had to admit, it probably didn't. I was culpable, there was no denying it, but I wanted to right my mistakes. If Holly had taught me anything, it was that.

"I'm sorry, I never meant for anything to happen — it just did." I paused, running a hand through my hair, trying to package my wrongdoing into something palatable. "But we didn't sleep together." I bit my lip. "When did she tell you?"

"She didn't — you just did."

Ah.

"I went through her phone and put two and two together. I confronted her, but she claimed it was nothing. But I'm not sticking around for that. I've already had one failed marriage, I don't need my second starting off on the wrong foot."

I was confused. "Wait — so you're not getting married now?"

Melanie shook her head. "Nope. I dumped her over the weekend after I found this out. If I can't trust her, I don't want her. So actually, you did me a favour, which is why I've decided to spare you." She shook her head. "I should be thanking you for exposing her for what she is, but I'm not quite at that stage yet."

Melanie had dumped Nicola Sheen — I hadn't seen that one coming. And while she'd done the right thing, it didn't stop me feeling sorry for Nicola. That meant she was back to square one, single and living with her parents. But that was her choice, her life. I had mine now and I was more than happy with it.

I waved my hand around the store. "So have you come for a spot of retail therapy?" I asked Melanie.

"Something like that," she said. "I actually just came to return all of Nicola's wedding and Christmas gifts. And now that's done, I feel a lot better. I wanted it to work, but I knew something wasn't right." Melanie looked me in the eye. "So you're welcome to her. But I pity you if she's your ultimate love, that's all I'll say."

I spluttered. "She's not my ultimate love." It felt like I was being unfaithful to Holly even having this conversation.

"You could have fooled me. I read some of those texts you know."

I'd never said anything close to that I was sure, but it didn't stop my cheeks turning the colour of a robin's breast. Is there anything more embarrassing than friends reading your personal, private text messages? Melanie might as well have watched a sex tape. The atmosphere was so thick, you could slice it.

"I certainly never said that — whatever Nicola and I had is definitely in the past. And I am sorry, truly I am. I shouldn't have kissed her, but it just happened."

"Your mouth slipped and fell on her face?"

When she put it like that. "Something like that," I mumbled. Then I cleared my throat. "I'm sorry it ended like this for you."

Melanie sighed and shrugged. "Like I said, you did me a favour. And now you don't want her either — looks like Nicola's the one to lose out, isn't it?"

I nodded. "Looks like."

We stared at each other, and then Melanie glanced down at my shopping basket with my knitted Christmas decoration sitting pretty, ready to be purchased. She bent down and picked it up, before glancing at me.

"You've moved on already? 'Our First Christmas'?" She shook her head. "You don't mess around do you?"

Now I *really* wanted to get away from Melanie as quickly as possible.

"Who's the lucky lady?" There was definite sarcasm in her voice. "Anyone I know?"

"No," I said, shaking my head. "It's not for me, it's a Christmas present."

I wasn't prepared to tell anybody about Holly just yet. It was far too new and precious to share with the rest of the world.

Melanie put the decoration back in my basket and hoisted her handbag high on her shoulder. "Well, have a great Christmas, Tori." She stepped forward into my personal space. "And a word of friendly advice — if you want to stay safe, try not to fall on to anyone else's girlfriend's face, okay?"

I swallowed hard as Melanie glared into my eyes. There were so many responses forming in my head, but I decided to say nothing. Being threatened in this setting was already surreal enough.

I let out a long breath as Melanie turned on her heel and walked away from me. I plucked my new decoration from my basket and hot-footed it to the till before anybody else cornered me and threatened violence. Suddenly, this department was not such a sanctuary of hope and glitter.

Now, I just wanted to get home, bolt the door and have a stiff glass of red wine.

22

Tuesday December 20th

I was lying on top of Holly on the sofa, still inside her. I moved my fingers slowly and she exhaled, closing her eyes, clutching on to me. I could see she was still falling, still recovering from our most recent sexual encounter.

It had all started when I walked in the door from work around 6pm and Holly was sitting on the couch.

She'd smiled at me, not having any idea how irresistible she was.

I'd walked over to her, full of intent, and kissed her.

Fifteen minutes later, here we were.

I kissed her neck and pushed myself in deeper. I never wanted to leave. I had no idea what I'd done before this point in my life or what I might do afterwards, but none of that mattered. The only important thing was that I was inside Holly, she was mine and I was going nowhere.

She opened one eye and saw me staring.

I shot her a wicked grin.

"You think we could go about our daily lives in this position?" she asked, smirking.

"I'm willing if you are."

"We may as well give it a go."

I moved my fingers again and she pushed her head back into a cushion.

"Can't see any drawbacks at all, can you?" she asked, her voice croaky.

I shook my head, feeling gallons of emotion well up inside me. "None at all," I said, pressing my lips to hers.

***

Two hours later and we were laying on the bed, the sugar rush of sex still coursing through our veins. My stomach rumbled as I lay beside her, one leg slung lazily over her thigh.

"You hungry?" She smoothed back some hair from my forehead.

"Seeing as I haven't eaten since lunchtime, I think probably yes."

Holly leaned back and grabbed her phone from the bedside table. She swiped the screen and the light made her squint. "Half eight," she said. "We could order in. Or we could go out, go to that new Thai place down the road." She put the phone on the table and rolled back, taking me in her arms and placing a kiss on the side of my neck. "You up for something spicy?"

I laughed. "That's why we haven't eaten properly for

the past few days," I said. "Anyway, going out? I'm not sure I'd make it that far."

"True," Holly replied. "Shall I order a pizza then?"

I nodded. "Sounds perfect." I kissed her again. I couldn't stop. I wanted to make every second count, seeing as I'd spent the last 16 years not kissing her.

She gave me a quizzical look. "What's going on inside your head right now?"

"Why?"

"Because you have a really weird look on your face. Like you're thinking about something and it's hurting your brain."

I shifted my position to stop my arm going dead. "Do I look gorgeous?"

Holly smiled. "You look constipated."

I let out a loud laugh. "You see, this is the downside of getting together with someone you know — you would never normally say that to a girl on your second date."

Holly grinned her lopsided smile. "Is this our second date? I just thought we'd muddled through a few days not leaving our beds. I wasn't aware we'd ever actually had a date."

I rolled on to my back and thought about that. "You know what, you're absolutely right. We haven't had a date."

"We'd have to leave the flat and everything," Holly said.

I waved a finger in the air. "Definite downside." I leaned forward and kissed her, and the spark rolled down my body, down to my toes, then back up to my clit.

I really didn't want to get up. But it wasn't as if we couldn't come back to this very spot later, now was it?

I pushed myself up on my elbows, then hopped out of bed. I stepped into my pants and jeans, and when I turned around, Holly's expression spelled alarm.

"What?" I asked. I walked over and threw back the covers. "Come on, chop-chop. We're going out on a date. Our very first date, in fact." I bent over, picked up her jeans and threw them at her. "Get dressed, wench, we're hitting the town."

In response, Holly simply pulled up the duvet cover over her head and groaned.

I pulled it back down. "I'm going to splash my face and wash my hands. I suggest you do the same. Especially your hands because I know exactly where they've been."

I knew that would draw a massive grin.

I was right.

***

We made it out of the flat 20 minutes later and were sat in Baker's Bar by 9.15pm, burgers ordered, craft beer in front of us.

"I ordered you a Christmas beer — Rudolph's Ruby Ale."

I took a sip. It was bitter, but I smiled anyway. Maybe I would get used to the taste eventually. Or maybe I could tell Holly I'd stick to red wine in about a week, when I was sure things had settled down. Not that I thought she was going anywhere, but there was still beginning-of-relationship protocol to follow.

"What did you get?" I asked.

"Cranberry Porter — want to try?" She held out her beer to me, but I shook my head. The colour alone was enough to put me off, resembling what I imagined Rudolph's blood might look like on a particularly cold day.

Holly took a sip and leaned back, grinning at me.

"What?" I wrinkled my nose.

"Us. This." Holly stretched out her long legs so her feet were lounging beside my chair. "I'm still getting used to it. In a good way."

A waft of barbecued meat drifted into the bar and my stomach rumbled. "Let's hope they don't burn the kitchen down and Nicola has to rescue us. That'd be just my luck."

Holly laughed. "I think that's the smell of burgers cooking, not being burnt."

I took a sip of my beer and flexed my jaw. "Talking of Nicola," I said.

Holly raised an eyebrow. "I didn't think we were."

I leaned over and planted a kiss on her lips.

"Well, nearly Nicola. I was out shopping yesterday and I ran into Melanie. In Selfridges' Christmas department."

Holly covered her mouth as she sat up straight. "Your sacred place," she said.

I nodded. "Anyway, turns out, this isn't going to be such a happy Christmas for Nicola."

Holly looked nonplussed. "She lost you, so I'd say that was obvious."

I drew in a sharp breath. This 'girlfriend' side of Holly was all new to me, and it was still taking me by surprise. A nice surprise, but still — I wasn't used to her waxing lyrical about me.

"You're pretty sweet, you know that?"

She dipped her eyes and gave me a bashful smile.

"Anyway, Melanie's dumped Nicola — the wedding's off."

Holly's mouth dropped open. "Really?" she said. "Well I never. Even Melanie has standards that Nicola didn't reach. That is damning in the extreme."

I didn't say anything, just fiddled with my napkin. I thought Holly was being a little harsh, but said nothing. Old habits died hard where Nicola Sheen was concerned.

"But let's consign Nicola to the backburner, shall we?" Holly said.

"Backburner? Really?"

Holly laughed. "That was not intentional." She paused. "But you know what I mean. No more talk of Nicola or Melanie. Let's just concentrate on us, because we're far more interesting. Me and you, Christmas, our party, my birthday — it's going to be amazing."

"I hope so. How many have we got coming to the party?"

"I think about 20 last count, which is perfect."

"Agreed. And we're doing those mince pie martinis?"

"We are."

"Great. And the Dixie Chicks tomorrow too."

Holly licked her lips and nodded. "It's going to be the perfect Christmas. Well, the lead-up is, anyway."

"It is," I said. "You know the only thing that would make it more perfect?"

Holly thought for a moment. "A kitten?"

I laughed. "That goes without saying — *everything's* made better by a kitten. I was wondering if you'd thought about spending Christmas at mine? I wanted you to come before all of this, and now it just seems weird we might be apart."

Holly winced before she spoke, which was never a great sign. "I know." She held up her hand to stop me butting in. It worked. "And I have been thinking about it, even before anything happened between us." She trailed her finger up and down her glass. "I'm still thinking about whether I can take the fallout from my parents, or if they'd even notice I'm not there." She shrugged. "Leave it with me, okay?"

I knew being in the middle of her parents' constant tug of war was no fun for Holly and I felt for her. But I also wanted her to make herself happy too, rather than putting up with the same situation every year.

"It's less than a week away," I said.

She fixed me with a stare.

I held up my hands and smiled. "I'll leave it with you."

23

Friday December 23rd

Last night, Holly and I had gone to see the Dixie Chicks and it had been just about perfect. I'd bagged fabulous seats and Holly was in her element, the only thing missing being a Stetson and cowboy boots. Being under 30, we were the youngest people there by some distance, but the lesbian contingent as ever was front and centre, which made it all the more special. We'd left the concert tired and elated, then come home to bed with each other. We were still getting to know each other, still getting attuned to each other's bodies, and that was cool. We had all the time in the world.

This morning, Holly had left early — she had a client breakfast. I'd been aghast at the concept, especially on December 23rd, but Holly said this was a corporate client taking her out to say thanks for all of her help throughout the year so she couldn't say no. But honestly, getting people out of bed when they were in the first throes of a relationship? It was just plain rude.

I, on the other hand, was in the opposite camp. I was working from home today, the final day of work before the Christmas break and I had a party to prep for. It was all hands on deck — so long as those hands were mine.

But sitting here now, with my first coffee of the morning, there was an odd feeling swelling within me. I watched the trains rattling by, revelling in the order they brought to the day and tried to pinpoint it. And then it struck me. I was content, happy. And after such a drama-packed December, that was a gorgeous revelation.

It was December 23rd. On November 25th, on that hilltop with Holly, I'd laid out my plan to get a girlfriend before Christmas. I'd been gung-ho, up for the fight, ready to go into battle. And battle I had — through bizarre sex, through insurance scams, through first loves magically appearing. But I'd made it through to the other side, and I'd found a girlfriend I never imagined. At least, I hoped she was my girlfriend. We hadn't discussed the G word yet.

As if sensing I was thinking about her, my phone beeped on the sofa beside me and I picked it up. It was Holly.

'Morning. Just thought I'd let you know I'd rather still be in bed with you even though this breakfast is delicious. But you're more tasty. X' She'd attached an image of her eggs benedict, replete with coffee, orange juice and champagne.

I smiled goofily at the phone, then rolled my eyes at myself.

Holly. It was Holly all along. All these years, all this time. But would it have worked sooner? I'm not sure. Maybe it took me till this point to see that what I'd been searching for was right in front of me from the very start. Tall, gorgeous, reliable Holly, with legs as long as the M1. Never again would it be a problem painting a ceiling.

I took another slug of my coffee, then grabbed a pen and paper from the kitchen counter. There was a lot to do today, a party to prep for. And it had to be fabulous with Holly as the star guest.

Plus, we were debuting our relationship tonight to our friends. I was a little nervous about how it would all go down.

***

"I can't believe you two have finally got together — you took your time!"

I was standing in front of Holly's friend Daisy, who I'd met last year at the Christmas bash. Her girlfriend Jasmine was with her, and they'd brought a spectacular bunch of birthday flowers that I was currently holding — Holly had dashed off to find a suitable vase.

"Didn't want to rush into anything," I replied. Had everyone known we should be together and not told us?

"Daisy and I had a bet it would happen when she met you last year at the Christmas party, didn't we?"

Daisy nodded. "I thought you were a couple already till Jas put me right."

"Did you?" This was a new one.

"Uh-huh. Just something about the way you were so comfortable around each other, anticipating the other's needs, the looks Holly gave you." She shrugged. "I just assumed, but Jas corrected me. But I knew I was right!"

I smiled at her. "Well done, I think?" I looked around the room. "I've no idea where Holly is right now though."

Looking over my shoulder, Jasmine raised an eyebrow and gave a slight splutter. "I think I do."

I turned my head and now I saw Holly. Doing her best impression of a modern Santa, wearing bright red velvet trousers, a white shirt, red velvet jacket and a bow tie hanging loosely around her neck. Her green eyes sparkled in the party atmosphere, and her hair was shaped to one side. She was also carrying a tall vase for the flowers.

On sight, every nerve ending in my body jangled. This woman was my girlfriend. The universe could be very kind sometimes.

Gaining wolf whistles as she walked through the lounge and deposited the vase on the counter, Holly took the flowers from me, filled the vase and arranged them. Then she stood back to admire her handy work.

"Pretty good?" she asked.

"You're a natural," I told her.

She put the flowers on the window sill, then came back to my side, snaking an arm around my waist.

"I'm here to stay this time," Holly said. "I haven't seen you in ages," she told Jasmine, touching her arm.

"Far too long," Jasmine said. "And now look at you — you've got a brand new girlfriend and you've raided Austin Powers' wardrobe."

Holly let out a bark of indignation. "Austin Powers? I think I look a little cooler than that." She gave us a twirl before looking at me. "I was going for something Christmassy, I'm not sure what. Maybe one of Santa's taller, sexier, slightly butch helpers?"

I put my arm around Holly's waist this time. "You look hot, whatever you are."

"How are things with you guys?" Holly asked.

Jasmine and Daisy radiated matching grins.

"Perfect," Jasmine said. "We're hosting Boxing Day for mine and Daisy's families, so that'll be interesting. Fifteen adults and four kids in our flat — did we think this through?"

Daisy elbowed her girlfriend. "It's going to be fine and if it's not, we'll just get them drunk."

"Sounds like a perfect plan," Holly said. "Talking of which, can I top up your drinks?"

We all agreed and Holly turned towards the kitchen.

***

The evening went off with a festive bang, the mince pie martinis going down a storm. Once they'd run out, we moved on to wine, beer and Prosecco, cranking up the

Christmas tunes to get everyone in the party mood. Our friends didn't need much persuasion. Plus, with our newly purchased patio heater roaring into action, our balcony was suddenly a destination, with train passengers waving at us as they passed. Christmas fever is infectious, my dad taught me that.

Around midnight, we toasted in Christmas Eve and Holly put on Mariah Carey's 'All I Want For Christmas Is You' — she knew it was my all-time favourite Christmas tune. We danced around our lounge pointing and singing at each other with the rest of our friends, but my eyes were only ever on Holly. This Christmas, she *was* all I wanted and all my dreams *had* come true. Turns out, Mariah was prophetic.

The last guest cleared out around 3am, and we took a couple of glasses of Prosecco out on to the balcony to stare at the stars. Well, that was the plan, but the light pollution in London spoilt the intention. We could see a few sparkling lights in the inky canvas overhead, but whether they were planes, drones or stars, we weren't sure.

A few moments later, Holly clicked her fingers together. "I almost forgot." She dipped into the pocket of her red jacket and produced a sprig of mistletoe.

I grinned at her. "You old smoothie."

She winked, before holding it over our heads and kissing me softly.

I melted on the spot. Holly's lips were so warm and

inviting, I was happy to pull up a chair and stay all night. Eventually though, she pulled away.

"Happy Christmas Eve, beautiful," she said. "And happy anniversary!" Holly held up her glass to cheers.

I clinked mine to hers. "It's our anniversary?"

She nodded. "One week today." She paused. "And what a week it's been." She shot me her lopsided smile. "Thanks for getting everything ready for today too, I really do appreciate it."

"The least I could do for my new girlfriend," I said. Then I held my breath. Shit. I hadn't meant that to just slip out. I flicked my gaze up to Holly who was grinning.

"Girlfriend? You don't mess around, do you?"

"It just came out — we don't have to be yet if you're not ready. I won't be upset." I wanted to lower my eyebrows, but they were stuck in an alarmed position on my face.

"You won't?" Holly stepped forward and gathered me in her arms, looking down into my eyes.

I swallowed and shook my head. "Just an expression, I didn't mean it seriously."

The corners of Holly's mouth tugged upwards. "Tori, I've been your girlfriend since we kissed on the kitchen floor. I'm not going anywhere. So just relax, okay?"

I nodded, still not trusting myself to speak again.

Holly put both our glasses on the floor, re-gathered me in her arms and kissed me with utter intent. I was floored, but also wrapped in her warmth — metaphorically and literally. When she kissed me, strange things happened. That much I knew.

Within seconds, she lifted me on to our small balcony table and hitched up my skirt. I took a sharp intake of breath. The mood had just turned up a notch and I smiled as I saw the lust pooling in Holly's eyes.

"Not too cold?" Holly asked, never taking her mouth from mine.

I shook my head, feeling a rush between my legs in anticipation.

Holly's body moved forwards and she spread my legs, moving her tongue inside my mouth.

I groaned.

She ran her hands up and down my sides while she deepened our kiss further, then her hand grazed my thighs.

She was going to fuck me on this table, in the open air. In that second, I didn't think it was possible to love anybody more than I did right then, and that thought made me open my eyes.

Holly's hand reached up and tugged off my pants, pushing up my bum so I could wriggle out of them. A fresh gust of air hit me as I sat back down and we retook our positions. Now Holly's hand was hot over my pussy, her mouth in front of mine.

"Okay?" she asked, biting my lip and slipping a finger inside me. "I've been wanting to do this all night long."

I went to reply but nothing came out. I was too lost in her, lost in the moment, overtaken by Holly.

She slipped in another finger and I groaned, pushing my hips forward, feeling freer now than I had in years. Sex had always been high on my agenda, but I hadn't had sex with someone I felt so attuned to in quite a while.

What's more, nobody had ever taken me on a balcony before, so Holly was winning hands-down.

I put my mouth beside Holly's ear, my breath wispy. "If you're going to fuck me, just do it," I said.

She didn't need a second invitation.

As her fingers began moving back and forth, my mouth dropped open but the December air that coated my throat felt warm and inviting. I threw my arms around Holly's neck and opened my legs, welcoming her in, encouraging her to go further.

She shifted as close as she could get and slid her tongue into my mouth as she went deeper.

I clung on for the ride of my life as our bodies melded into one.

She ramped up her festive charm offensive, slipping and sliding all around me, over me, inside me — I loved being in her orbit. With every second that passed, we grew more urgent, Holly with laser-like focus, mine more hazy as the thunder in my body built. She hit my G-spot and I groaned into her mouth, before flinging my head backwards.

In return, I heard her grin.

I began seeing stars and wasn't sure if they were fake or real. I was on the edge, staring at the universe, shouting out its name. Or it could well have been Holly's name. I was wrapped around her, pressing into her. Holly was everything I asked for on my Christmas list and way more besides.

I was so close, then Holly put her mouth beside my ear. "Come for me, or you'll be on the naughty list," she said.

My muscles spasmed, and I dug my fingers into Holly's neck while she swiped her thumb back and forth.

I did as I was told, coming in a hot rush all over her fingers, shouting into the darkness for all I was worth.

But Holly didn't let up and within seconds I was coming again, shouting again, feeling wild abandon cascading from my very core.

Holly kissed my neck, my ear, my hair, my mouth. Every connection made me jolt, my nerves on high alert to this emotional tour de force. She held me close while I steadied my breath, my arms flung around her neck, clinging to my anchor. When I leaned back and found her gaze, we were both grinning like idiots.

I kissed Holly hard, wanting to show her everything I was feeling. But even I knew that was hard to sum up in one kiss. I was still flying and I wanted to take Holly with me too.

I reached for her zip, but she caught my hand and held on to it. I pulled back, searching her eyes with mine.

Holly just smiled a lazy smile as she extracted her hand from me.

I let my eyelids droop lazily.

She kissed my lips. "Shall we take this inside?" Her breath was hot against my ear and tingled down my entire body. Inside was probably a very good idea.

I grinned at her. "When I regain the use of my legs, absolutely," I said, pressing my lips to hers again.

24

Saturday December 24th

We got up around 1pm the following day, cleared up the flat and then sat smiling at each other. I didn't recall doing this with anybody else I'd been with, so I was either turning into someone I didn't recognise, or I was falling in love — truly in love — for the very first time. I was pretty sure it was the latter.

Holly made me a cup of coffee and we sat on the sofa eating leftover pepperoni pizza from the night before. It always tasted better the next day, and this afternoon was no exception.

"I don't want you to go today. It's going to feel like I've lost a limb." I stared at her.

"I know."

"So stay. Call your Mum and come with me tomorrow. We can spend our first Christmas together."

Holly sighed and chewed on some pizza. She sipped her tea and stared out the window at the afternoon winter sun. The trains were still chugging past, although we expected that to stop soon, being it was Christmas Eve, when everything came to a standstill around 5pm.

All I wanted for Christmas was sitting on the sofa staring at me. And preparing to leave me.

"Don't look so sad," I said, reaching across and kissing Holly's hand. "I didn't mean to make you sad."

Holly smiled. "You haven't made me sad, believe me." She curled her long legs up under her body and sighed. "It's just… a bit late to tell my parents I'm not coming, that's all. They're expecting me."

I squeezed her arm. "I know — I'm just being a selfish brat." I paused. "Go, and we'll see each other the day after, or the one after that." I smiled to back up my last statement. "It's just, I'm not going to be able to function without you." I put my head in my hands. "And will you stop me talking such drivel? I've turned into one of those snivelling wrecks and it's your fault."

She laughed and put my feet on her lap, massaging one of them up, then down. "Whatever it is, you've turned me into it too." She paused. "But let's not focus on negatives today. We've got the rest of the day together, so let's do something fun. How about we have a walk around the Christmas lights in town, like your parents always used to do when you were little?"

My heart swelled so much inside my chest, I thought it might burst out at any second. This was the love I'd read about, the love I'd hoped for. It's one thing to wish for a

Christmas girlfriend. It's quite another for her to arrive and be so utterly, deliciously perfect.

"I would love that," I replied, beaming at Holly. "You really know how to sweep a girl off her feet, you know that?"

She squeezed my foot. "I've got skills," she said. "It's settled then. We can eat hot dogs and roasted chestnuts from those dodgy street carts, have mulled wine and be so Christmassy, your teeth will ache."

"Sounds like my ideal date."

I leaned back, never taking my eyes off of Holly. "You know, when I started my girlfriend quest on November 25th, I wanted three things: a girlfriend, drunk Christmas sex and a present from someone who wasn't related to me." I paused. "But that was Tori 1.0. Unreformed Tori. Naughty Tori."

"I think you're still a bit naughty," Holly replied, grinning.

"I've got skills too," I winked. "But things have changed. I've changed. It's like I told you in the beginning — I didn't really want anything, I wanted *someone*. But the someone I ended up with is so much more than I bargained for. I had a plan, I had dreams and goals, but you've shifted the goalposts. Now you're a part of those dreams." I paused. "You are those dreams."

Holly's cheeks reddened and she looked down. "Are you trying to make me blush?" she asked.

I smiled. "I'm not, but I can't keep this quiet. I feel so

loved, so cared for, so *safe*. And that would never have happened so quickly if it hadn't been you because I knew you already." Tears threatened but I held them in. They were happy tears, but I didn't want any mixed messages.

I took Holly's hand in mine and kissed her silky fingers. "You're more than I ever dreamed of, you know that?" I whispered. "I'm already in love with you."

I couldn't contain my emotions around Holly. My mouth just ran away with me. Everything about us was just so huge and overwhelming, I had emotions leaking out of every pore.

"Does that scare you?" I asked.

Holly flipped my feet off of her lap and scooted across the sofa, taking me in her arms. The kiss she gave me started on my lips, but vibrated right down to my toes. When she pulled back, her eyes were large pools of happiness, shimmering in the afternoon light.

"Last night you call me your girlfriend, now you tell me you love me. What's tomorrow's declaration?"

"Happy birthday?" I said, smiling. Then I paused. "So does it?" I asked again.

Holly crinkled her face. "What?"

"Scare you?"

She shook her head and kissed me again lightly. "Don't be stupid. I've loved you for years. Taking the leap to being *in love* with you happened weeks ago. There's no getting away from me now, I'm here to stay."

Relief washed over me. Holly loved me.

I moved my head and stared right at her. "You sure?"

She tilted her head. "Positive," she replied. "I know it's only been a week, but it's been way longer really, hasn't it? We just feel so right, you and me." She shrugged. "We just are."

I put my head on Holly's chest and we sat like that for a few moments, the gentle hum of the trains buzzing by. In that moment, we were cocooned, untouchable, in love. She kissed the top of my head and I was content to ride the rise and fall of her body, warmth emanating from her.

It seemed like for once, I'd landed right where I belonged.

25

Christmas Day

I woke up the next day and my eyes shot open — it was Christmas Day! Then a wave of tiredness washed over me as I checked my phone. It was also 7am. My body clock hadn't got used to waking up late yet, it was still on work time. On top of that, my bed was empty.

Holly had gone to her Mum's house late last night after a magical afternoon walking hand-in-hand around the West End Christmas lights. Being there with Holly as my girlfriend had made it extra-special, and the whole way round, I'd felt like my dad was with us, our very own Christmas spirit guiding us on our way.

Now, Holly would be getting ready for her annual birthday breakfast with both her parents. This was their concession for their Christmas baby — they couldn't stand the thought of spending Christmas Day together, but Christmas breakfast for Holly, they could handle.

I hoped it went okay, although I knew Holly's mum

was always anxious on Christmas Eve in the lead-up to it. Holly had already told me that this year would be the last time they all put themselves through it. She'd wanted to stop it years ago, but her parents were adamant they wanted to do it for her. But now, aged 28, she'd had enough. Plus, her dad had a new partner and baby, so he had other commitments to attend to.

Holly much preferred to see her parents separately, where she claimed they were bearable, albeit in small doses.

As I was up, I decided to get going — there was nothing to stick around the flat for, and I had a suitcase and presents to pack. I turned on the radio and cranked up the volume — it was playing 'Last Christmas'. I jumped in the shower, positivity crackling in my veins. This year, I'd followed George Michael's advice to a tee and given my heart to someone special.

Perhaps I should search the entire back catalogue of Wham! for the answers to all of life's pressing issues.

***

Traffic on Christmas Day was non-existent and my drive home was one of my favourite journeys of the year, singing along to Christmas tunes on the radio all the way. To zip down roads normally clogged with traffic was almost miraculous, and always made me feel like I was in a pop video. Today, the air was crisp with anticipation, the sun sitting low, the clouds lounging casually across the skyline. My drive took just over an hour, and I pulled up outside my mum's front door on the outskirts of Oxford just before ten — she was going to faint when she saw me this early.

I checked my phone to see if Holly had replied to my good morning text and saw I had a message. I clicked on it smiling. My smile quickly turned to a frown.

'Happy Christmas — hope it's a fab one! Love, Nicola. X'

I stared at the phone. This was clearly one of those 'text everyone in my phone' messages, the modern-day equivalent of the Christmas card letter. But couldn't she have left me out of the loop? Surely she could have unchecked me and Melanie from her list? That thought made my heart stop thumping so hard in my chest. If this rattled me, imagine the impact on Melanie Taylor.

I closed my eyes and took a deep breath. That was all in the past, and Holly was now my future. Sweet, sexy, gorgeous Holly. An image of her taking me on the balcony popped into my brain and I shivered. Now I just had to get that out of my brain before I knocked on my mum's front door. It used to be my parents' front door, but now, it was just my mum's. I wasn't sure I'd ever get used to that.

I stepped out of my hired Renault and pulled my coat around me, checking the sky. It was freezing, cold enough to snow even. That would make it the most perfect Christmas ever.

The front door was open before I got there with Mum

standing in her Christmas apron, fluffy slippers on, face already flushed from the cooking marathon.

"You're early," she said. "Happy Christmas, kiddo."

I set down my case and gave her a hug.

"Happy Christmas to you, too."

Mum peered over my shoulder. "No Holly?"

I shook my head. "Family duty."

Mum picked up my suitcase and pulled me in, but I pulled back.

"Let me just get the presents." I indicated over my shoulder and she nodded.

"I'll put the kettle on," she shouted.

Ten minutes later and I was sitting at the table in Mum's bright kitchen, her well-tended garden shivering through the window in the winter air. Freshly baked mince pies were cooling on wire trays, veg was prepped and floating in water, and a Christmas ham was glazed and steaming on a wooden board.

I sipped my tea and took in the familiar scene from my childhood. Everything was just the same, apart from one crucial missing person.

"What time did you get up this morning? This makes me look lazy."

Mum smiled. "You know me — I'm an early bird. Plus, nothing excites me like Christmas morning, so I like to enjoy as much of it as I can!" She gave me a squeeze and a kiss. "This was always your dad's favourite morning too, you know."

"Dad loved every morning in December."

She smiled. "He did, didn't he?" A pause. "God, I miss him."

I squeezed her back. Dad's absence at this time of year was like an open wound, one that would never heal. We just had to patch it up the best way we knew how and make this the best Christmas ever in his honour. We wouldn't ever forget him, so it seemed appropriate to include him in whatever we did.

"I know. I miss him too." My mouth twitched. "But that's why I love Christmas so much, Dad's love of it was infectious. Which is why I hate that Holly has to have a sad one, on her birthday too. I wish there was something I could do."

Mum shot me a sympathetic glance. "Families have to do their own traditions. You can make new ones soon for yourself, you'll see. And have I told you how happy I am you're with Holly?"

I smiled up at her. "I might have got that impression when you screamed down the phone."

"Well I am. She's wonderful. She's everything I could ever have hoped for my darling daughter."

I grinned up at her. "For once in our lives when it comes to my love life, we're in total agreement."

Mum brushed her hand across my cheek. "And you're looking good on it too — glowing. I remember glowing when I first met your father, everybody said so." She gave me a wistful smile. "Glowing is good, kiddo, so cherish it.

Hold on to the person who makes you glow. They're few and far between."

I caught my mum's hand and kissed it. "I intend to hold on to her," I replied.

If Holly and I could be anything like my mum and dad, that would make us an incredible love story.

I already knew we stood a fighting chance.

***

The first eggnogs had been demolished, the turkey was resting and dinner was a mere half hour from being served. Gran and Aunty Ellen were busy peering at their new fitness trackers attached to their wrists — Mum's present to them both.

"So it monitors your steps, your calorie intake and your sleep?" Gran was tapping it, and every time it lit up, her face went into delighted mode.

"It does," I told her.

"But how does it know what I've eaten?" Gran held up her wrist and peered all around her present. "Does it have a camera on it recording me?"

Mum laughed. "You have to log your food in your iPhone, Mum. I gave you my old one, so you've got one of those."

"Right." Gran put her mouth to her wrist. "Hello?" she said.

Mum sighed. "It can't hear you."

Gran winked. "I'm having you on," she replied. "So

it's called a Fitvit?" She paused. "What does the 'VIT' stand for, I wonder?"

"Very important person, Jill. Are you stupid?" That was Aunt Ellen chiming in.

"VIT, not VIP. And who are you calling stupid?" Gran nudged Ellen with her elbow.

"It's FitBIT, not VIT," Mum said. "Fit*bit*."

"Aaah!" both sisters chorused.

I burst out laughing. "You should take this on the road, you know. I've said it before and I'll say it again."

Gran smiled at me. "We should. But I don't want to show Ellen up as being the dull sister, and that's just what would happen." She sat back and grinned at her sister.

"Dull? Who's the one sitting around perfecting her Bridge game, while I'm touring the world?" Ellen crossed her arms and harrumphed at Gran.

It was Christmas as usual, with the Robinson sisters fighting for omnipotence. Having no siblings, I had no idea if this is what I'd be like with a sister, but it'd always fascinated me that Gran still quarrelled with hers into her 70s.

The front doorbell interrupted the family moment.

"Will you get that?" Mum asked.

I pushed back my chair. "Who the hell's coming round at 2pm on Christmas Day?"

Mum just smiled at me oddly.

I could still hear Gran and Ellen's chatter as I pulled open the door.

And when I did, my mouth dropped open.

Standing on the other side was Holly and her mum, loaded down with bags and presents.

"Special delivery," Holly said, smiling so much she looked like she might burst at any second. She'd styled her jet black hair slightly differently, and it fell delectably across her face.

My heart leapt into my mouth and a thousand stars exploded in front of my eyes. I blinked and hoped I wasn't about to faint. Holly was drop dead gorgeous.

"Are you going to let us in then, or is there a special password?"

I stood back and Holly stepped into the house, giving me a brief kiss on the lips. The world swayed back and forth in my vision.

"And close your mouth, drooling is not a good Christmas look," she said.

I pasted a smile on my face as Holly's mum, Gina, walked in.

"Happy Christmas!" she trilled, a little too brightly.

"You too!" I gave her a kiss on the cheek and heard a wave of greetings as Holly and her mum walked through to the lounge.

I checked my hair in the hallway mirror, took a deep breath and followed them in.

***

"I can't believe you're here, but I'm so glad you are." I wrapped my arms around Holly's waist and pulled her down for a kiss. My head swam, but I was getting used to that. I'd dragged Holly into the kitchen to have a minute alone.

"I really missed you."

"Me too," she replied, pulling back. "But believe me, keeping this a secret has been hard work."

I stood back and pouted. "How long have you been cooking this up?"

She smiled. "Only since your mum called me on Thursday."

"You've known that long! But I've been badgering you to come here all week. Why didn't you say anything?" I was taken aback, albeit secretly impressed she'd managed to hold it in that long.

"Because then it wouldn't have been a surprise, would it?" Holly grinned at me. "Plus, I still had to go home for this morning. But this was the perfect solution, so well done to your mum."

"She's a sly one, I'll give her that."

Holly laughed. "She's a good one," she said, kissing me again. "Then I just had to work on my mum. But when I told her she didn't have to cook and that she'd have her own room for the night, she was surprisingly okay with it. Especially when I reminded her she liked your mum. It was almost like what I wanted on my birthday counted for something. Wonders will never cease."

I pursed my lips. "And how was she about us?"

Holly let out a bark of laughter. "Pretty much like everyone else — at last, etc."

"Wow, we were really slow to catch on, weren't we?"

Holly moved her head side to side. "Some were a little slower than others," she said, her voice sing-song.

I poked her in the ribs. "Alright smart-arse." Then I kissed her again, long and slow. When I pulled back, she had her lopsided grin pasted on her face.

"I don't think I'll ever tire of kissing your lips," she said, before pausing. "And no, I can't believe these things are coming out of my mouth either."

I smiled. "Don't worry, I was just thinking the same thing." I paused. "Happy birthday, by the way."

"Thanks, gorgeous," Holly said, before kissing me again.

And then my mum walked in, clapping her hands to announce her arrival. "Okay lovebirds, enough of that!"

We untangled ourselves and turned to see Mum and Gina smiling at us, dressed in identical grey jumpers.

"Why are you dressed the same?" Holly asked, before covering her mouth. "Shit, those are our presents, aren't they?"

"Not that they're not lovely, but was it buy one, get one free by any chance?" Mum was smiling as she said it. "They're ever so soft though, aren't they Gina?"

Gina put her sleeve to her face. "Like a baby's bum," she confirmed.

I started to laugh, as did Holly.

"Okay, in our defence, these were bought weeks ago and I never expected you to be opening them together. They were bought before we were even together," I said.

"We believe you, thousands wouldn't," Gina replied.

"They look great on you both, though," Holly said, styling it out.

I nodded to back her up. "Really good."

Mum gave Gina a nod. "Okay, we can take them off now. I think we've embarrassed our daughters enough." They chuckled as they took the jumpers off and put them on the sideboard.

Mum clapped her hands again to grab our attention. "Right, this is now officially operation Christmas and I need turkey carvers, vegetable carriers, potato wenches and all sorts of other jobs that I can't think of funny names for right at this moment. You in?"

I gave Mum a salute. "At your service, captain."

* * *

Christmas dinner was delicious, with Mum working her magic as she always did. As for Gina, well she really came out of her shell after her third glass of wine, telling us this was the best Christmas she'd had in years, and Holly agreed. When Mum invited them again for the following year, I thought Gina might sob with happiness.

And now Mum, Gina, Gran and Ellen were in the lounge watching *Love Actually*, while Holly and I had just finished clearing up the kitchen. Now she was pulling me up the stairs, into my bedroom, the one where we'd shared so many times as teenagers.

Only now, things were slightly different.

Holly sat me on the bed and then presented me with my present — it was a beautiful watch from Michael Kors.

"I love it," I told her, turning it over in my hand before putting it on my wrist. "Thank you." I tilted my head upwards and she leaned down and kissed me. "Is this what you bought me that day in town?"

Holly's cheeks coloured red. "I might have gone back and exchanged it for something a little more extravagant after what happened," she said.

"That's not in the rules," I replied, smiling. "And there was me, thinking I'd fallen for someone who could be trusted."

"You didn't change yours?"

I shook my head. "No, but I did buy you a bigger birthday present instead."

Holly rubbed her hands together and sat down beside me. "And have I told you, I can't wait to make some new Christmas memories in this bed tonight," she whispered in my ear.

I laughed as my ears turned red. "With both our mums in the house — ideal."

"It'll test your stealth powers," she replied, nibbling my earlobe.

"Anyway," I said, standing up and brushing Holly off. "Your presents. Here's what I bought in Selfridges that day." I put the present in her hands.

Holly ripped it open and gave me a broad smile when

she uncovered her new bag. "Just what I wanted. How did you know?"

I laughed. "I've no idea, apart from all those hints you kept dropping."

She reached out and grabbed my hand. "I love it, it's so soft." She stroked the leather. "Nearly as soft as your bum."

"That's the criteria I gave to the salesperson, so I'm glad you think so."

Then I leaned down with the jewellery box in my hand. "And this is for your birthday. I was going to drive over to yours tomorrow and surprise you, but no need for that now." I was inches from her face, looking into her deep green eyes. "Happy birthday." I kissed her and waited for her to open the gift.

This time, she was slow and considered, carefully undoing the Sellotape and then opening the box. When she saw the silver key necklace, she drew in a huge breath. Then she looked up at me, an epic smile splitting her face.

"It's perfect," she said. "Thank you." She put the necklace on straight away, then stood up and pressed her lips to mine. It was a wordless kiss, but it communicated the promise of so much more.

"Happy birthday, baby," I said. "And can I say, I'm so glad you're my Christmas girlfriend."

Holly smiled. "You do know that a girlfriend is for life though, right? Not just for Christmas? You can't leave me on the street in a month when you get bored of me."

"You better find a way to keep me interested then."

"I've got some ideas," she said, raising one eyebrow before pressing her hand between my legs.

I jolted in surprise.

"Girls, are you coming down?"

We both jolted this time. It was my mum, shouting up the stairs.

I rolled my eyes. "Be there in a minute!" I shouted. "And why does being in my room make me feel like we're 15 again? Tonight is going to be very weird."

"I can do weird too, if you want," Holly said, laughing.

I pulled her out on to the landing and she followed me down the stairs. I'd had a cheesy grin on my face most of the day and it was still there because today had been perfect, a Christmas surrounded by everyone I really loved. As we walked down the stairs, I could see flakes of snow falling outside the window.

"It's snowing!" I shrieked, rushing to the door and flinging it open. "It's snowing!" I repeated over my shoulder to Holly.

She walked up behind me, peered outside and then shut the door. "Yes, and it's freezing," she said, grabbing my hand and pulling me towards the lounge.

We pushed open the door to be greeted by Mum, Gran and Ellen letting off party poppers, and standing in front of them was Gina. She was holding a chocolate sponge birthday cake for Holly, lit with 28 candles. They began a chorus of 'Happy Birthday' and Holly looked bashful, all

6-foot-2 of her. When the song was done, she blew out the candles and we all clapped.

"Speech!" Gran said, wolf-whistling through her teeth.

Holly gave me an alarmed look.

"What?" I asked. "Whistling is one of Gran's super-powers."

"Very handy in a street fight too," Gran added helpfully.

Holly let out a nervous laugh.

"If you're not going to do a speech, I hope you at least made a wish before blowing out all of those candles," Gran continued.

"I hope you did too, love," Gina said, smiling at her daughter.

Holly's gaze, however, wasn't on Gran or her mum, but rather it was focused on me. She walked over to me and put an arm around my shoulders.

"So did you make a wish?" I asked.

Holly shook her head, before putting her mouth to my ear. "No need, they already came true."

I spluttered before looking up at her. "What did I say about you and your sweet talk?"

"That I'm the best at it?" she asked.

"You're a world beater," I replied.

THE END

Want more from me? Sign up to join my VIP Readers' Group and get a FREE lesbian romance, **It Had To Be You!** *Claim your free book here: www.clarelydon.co.uk/it-had-to-be-you*

My Christmas Favourites

Christmas Film
This is a straight toss-up between *The Holiday* (Kate Winslet & Cameron Diaz looking gorg) and *The Muppet Christmas Carol*. Because let's face it, the original Dickens was a bit dull, but added muppets = winner!

Christmas Tune
'Last Christmas' by Wham! takes it by a whisker, just ahead of The Pogues and Kirsty MacColl's 'Fairytale of New York'. Shout out for Phil Spector's 'A Christmas Gift For You' also, which is spectacular.

Christmas Food
Mince pies, with custard or Bailey's cream. Delish.

Christmas Drink
Mulled wine or mulled cider.

Christmas Present
'Now That's What I Call Music' Vol I. All those hits in one place? I was impressed.

Worst Christmas Present
A doll. A garlic baguette holder. A bottle of Sandalwood perfume. Thanks, Mum.

Christmas Decoration
Twinkly lights and mistletoe.

Christmas Event
Christmas markets! I heart Christmas markets! In the UK, Bath and Birmingham do them well. But mainland Europe does it better, natch.

Christmas Memory
Hiring Margate Youth Hostel for 5 days and spending Christmas there, along with nearly 50 of my family. Warm, fuzzy feelings!

Christmas Treat
Anything by Lindt. Reindeer, Santa, Snowman. I'm not fussy.

Did You Enjoy This Book?

If the answer's yes, I wonder if you'd consider leaving me a review wherever you bought it. Just a line or two is fine, and could really make the difference for someone else when they're wondering whether or not to take a chance on me and my writing. If you enjoyed the book and tell them why, it's possible your words will make them click the buy button, too! Just hop on over to wherever you bought this book — Amazon, Apple Books, Kobo, Bella Books, Barnes & Noble or any of the other digital outlets — and say what's in your heart. I always appreciate honest reviews.

Thank you, you're the best.

Love,
Clare x

Also by Clare Lydon

The All I Want Series
All I Want For Valentine's (Book 2)
All I Want For Spring (Book 3)
All I Want For Summer (Book 4)
All I Want For Autumn (Book 5)
All I Want Forever (Book 6)

Other Novels
A Taste Of Love
Before You Say I Do
Nothing To Lose: A Lesbian Romance
Once Upon A Princess
The Long Weekend
Twice In A Lifetime
You're My Kind

The London Romance Series
London Calling (Book 1)
This London Love (Book 2)
A Girl Called London (Book 3)
The London Of Us (Book 4)
London, Actually (Book 5)
Made In London (Book 6)

Printed in Great Britain
by Amazon